Caroline Anderson is a matriarch, writer, armchair gardener, unofficial tearoom researcher and eater of lovely cakes. Not necessarily in that order! What Caroline loves: her family. Her friends. Reading. Writing contemporary love stories. Hearing from readers. Walks by the sea with coffee/ice cream/cake thrown in! Torrential rain. Sunshine in spring/autumn. What Caroline hates: losing her pets. Fighting with her family. Cold weather. Hot weather. Computers. Clothes shopping. Caroline's plans: keep smiling and writing!

HEALING HER EMERGENCY DOC

CAROLINE ANDERSON

MILLS & BOON

First published in Great Britain 2021
by Mills & Boon, an imprint of HarperCollins*Publishers* Ltd,
1 London Bridge Street, London, SE1 9GF

www.harpercollins.co.uk

HarperCollins*Publishers*
1st Floor, Watermarque Building,
Ringsend Road, Dublin 4, Ireland

Large Print edition 2021

Healing Her Emergency Doc © 2021 Caroline Anderson

ISBN: 978-0-263-28811-7

11/21

MIX
Paper from
responsible sources
FSC™ C007454

This book is produced from independently certified FSC™ paper to ensure responsible forest management. For more information visit www.harpercollins.co.uk/green.

Printed and bound in the UK using 100% Renewable Electricity at CPI Group (UK) Ltd, Croydon, CR0 4YY

A massive thank-you
to all those people worldwide
who've put their lives on the line
to keep us safe and well and fed.
We owe you more than words can say.

CHAPTER ONE

'LAURA?'

The voice was deep, soft, and weirdly familiar. She hadn't heard it for years, but it still made her heart tumble in her chest.

No. It can't be...

But her heart was doing a little jig behind her ribs as if it knew better, and she felt suddenly dizzy and light-headed.

Don't be ridiculous. It's just low blood sugar. Or interview nerves. And anyway, it won't be him. Not here...

Slowly, reluctantly, she looked up and met those totally unforgettable slate grey eyes. Eyes that had teased, and laughed, and—just that once—burned for her.

But not now. Right now they looked a little stunned. She knew how that felt.

What's he doing here?

The interview? No—but why else would he be wearing a suit? And if he was in the running, she was scuppered. He was too good—too convincing. He should have been a salesman, not a doctor. He could convince anyone of anything, and the interview panel would fall for it, just like they all did. Like she had.

Almost… But she hadn't made it easy for him.

She'd turned him down over and over again for the whole of their medical degree course, but rejection had been a bit of a novelty for Tom 'Mr Popularity' Stryker and he wasn't a quitter, so it had turned into a sort of game. He'd ask, she'd say no.

It had taken him five years of persistence, but at the Leavers' Ball he'd had one last go, cranked up the charm to full volume and pulled out all the stops, and he'd almost convinced her to go home with him. Almost.

She hadn't seen him since that night, but just remembering it made her squirm. Awkward wasn't in it.

Please don't bring it up.

Surely he wouldn't, not here. Maybe he wouldn't. He was smiling at her now, the warm, effortlessly sexy smile that had always made her stomach turn over and her heart beat a little faster. So that hadn't changed, then.

Why aren't I over you?

Her breath locked in her throat, and she dredged up what was probably a very unconvincing smile and found her voice at last. 'Tom. What are you doing here?'

Stupid, inane question.

His mouth quirked, his smile wry now.

'Do I really need to answer that?'

She rolled her eyes. 'Probably not.'

He gave a soft huff of laughter, and dropped casually into the seat next to hers—not that there was a lot of choice as it was the only free seat in the small waiting area—and she shifted slightly away from him, because the scent drifting from his body brought back memories she would rather have forgotten.

Memories that had haunted her dreams for the last seven years while her imagination had tried to fill in the blanks.

'So, how are you?' he asked, and she swallowed.

'I'm...' What? Achingly lonely? A little lost since her grandfather died? Happy at work, but only then?

'I'm OK. Busy.' At least it wasn't a lie, although she'd be more OK if she could land this senior Specialty Registrar job in the Emergency Department she'd been working in for months, and he'd just messed that up for her. 'How about you?'

'Oh, I'm good,' he said. 'Busy, of course, like you, but it goes with the territory, I guess. So what have you been up to since uni? Presumably not married with three kids if you're going after a senior post.'

'No, no kids, I'm still single.' Or single again, since she'd dropped everything and come hotfoot to Suffolk, but she wasn't going to raise that, and anyway, she was more interested in him. 'How about you? Did you finally settle down?' she asked, to shift the conversation away from herself, and then regretted showing the slightest sign of curiosity. Not that she didn't want to know...

But his mouth tightened into what could barely be called a smile and those incredibly expressive eyes went blank.

'Oh, you know me, I'm a free spirit,' he said, his voice light and breezy and oddly unconvincing as he glanced away.

There was a whole world left unsaid, but he clearly didn't want to discuss it. Because he'd just come out of a messy relationship, too? She could understand that. She didn't want to talk about hers, either. They were both allowed their privacy, but it must have been pretty bad, because the Tom she knew would never leave London without a very good reason.

'So, where are you working now?' he asked, lobbing the ball firmly back into her court, but she wasn't about to tell him. On a need-to-know basis, he frankly didn't, and she wanted to keep this as impersonal as possible, so she stuck to the bare bones of the truth.

'Nowhere permanent at the moment. I've been doing a bit of locuming for a while, off and on.'

He frowned, his brows pleating together slightly as he looked back at her. 'Locuming? That doesn't sound like you. I thought you always wanted security?'

Trust him to get straight to the heart of it. She slapped on a smile and kept her voice deliberately light and airy as he'd done. 'I do, but I needed a break. I never had a gap year, so why not? But it's been nearly a year now, so it's probably time to get back to focusing on my career.'

He cocked his head on one side and studied her, looking unconvinced. 'You took a year out at this stage? Was that wise?'

She looked away. 'It was for me.'

'So is that what this is about, this interview? Getting back on track?'

'Pretty much,' she said, wondering when being economical with the truth morphed into a lie. 'Plus I need to earn a living and having a regular income is quite handy like that.'

He chuckled, suddenly looking more like the Tom she remembered, his eyes crinkling at the corners. They'd always done that, and she hated the effect it was having on her. That it had always had on her. 'So how about you?' she asked, still insanely curious about him leaving London. 'Why are you after this job in particular?'

He shrugged. 'Next step on the career ladder, nice place, good hospital—why not? Same reasons as you, I guess. So where are you living now?' he added, his breath drifting against her face, trailing over it like the touch of a feather and making all her nerve endings dance.

She ignored it, wondering what to tell him. Not too much. Not all of it. She settled on fact—economy with the truth again. 'At home—in my grandfather's house.'

He nodded slowly. 'That makes sense. How is he?'

She looked away, knowing her eyes would be raw with the pain of loss and really, really not wanting to go there. Not today of all days, with her interview looming. 'He's been ill, but he's—OK.' Now it's over...

The meeting room door opened and James, the ED clinical lead, ushered the first candidate out and looked round. 'Thomas Stryker?'

'Good luck,' she said mechanically, and he got to his feet.

'You know you don't mean that,' he murmured with a wry smile tugging at his ridiculously beautiful mouth, and turned towards James, the smile widening.

'Hi. I'm Tom.'

'James Slater. Come on in, Tom.'

The door to the meeting room closed behind them, and she stared at it, her shoulders slumping in despair.

He'll get it. He's bound to. Why didn't I do

*more interview prep? For all the difference
it'll make, with him in the running.*

That would teach her to take things for
granted, but she hadn't been alone. She'd
bumped into Matt Hunter yesterday when
he'd come down to the ED, and he'd wished
her luck. 'Livvy says you'll smash it,' he'd
told her, and she'd laughed. 'Your wife's just
being nice,' she'd told him, but he'd shaken his
head. 'No, she meant it. She says you're a great
doctor and a real asset to the department, and
James agrees. You'll get it, Laura. You're too
good to lose. We need people like you here.'

She'd believed him at the time, but not any
more. She looked at the other two candidates.
One looked terrified, the other bored and fidgety. The one who'd just come out had looked
near to tears. She might have stood a chance
against them, but now...

Now, there was Tom, always smiling, always
up for whatever challenge/opportunity/pretty
girl/party presented itself. He'd aced his medical degree, presumably sailed through the early
years of Foundation training and after another
five years was now a prime candidate for the

vacant senior SpR post in the ED at Yoxburgh Park Hospital. The role she'd hoped would be hers, the job she so desperately needed so she could stay here in her grandfather's house, with Millie.

The job she'd been told by James Slater to apply for, because it had her name written all over it.

Well, so it might have had, but James hadn't met Tom then, of course, and Tom had that way of convincing people that they wanted all sorts of things that in their right minds they wouldn't contemplate—although thankfully her common sense had rescued her from that particular catastrophe.

The door opened again, and her head snapped up. She could hear him laughing, hear the smile in his voice as he thanked them, almost smell the success on him as he walked confidently out of the room and took his seat again beside her.

'You look happy,' she said, forcing a smile, and he grinned.

'Well, I got through to the second round, so I'm not unhappy,' he said softly, and then

studied her searchingly, his brows pleating together. 'Are you OK?'

'Of course.' She looked away before he could
read the lie in her eyes. 'It's just a little—awkward. It's the last place I would have expected
you to look for a job.'

'Why? It's hardly outer Mongolia.'

'It's not London, either, so it just feels a bit
weird that you're here. It's not like you to go
provincial.'

She could feel him still studying her, his
eyes boring through into her brain, trying to
read her mind.

'It's not that that's bugging you. It's us.'

'There is—*was*—no us.'

The soft huff of his laugh drifted across her
skin, teasing her nerve endings.

'No, there wasn't, was there? And you're still
feeling guilty about that,' he murmured slowly,
and she could hear the laughter in his voice.

'Why should I feel guilty?' she muttered,
and she felt her skin tingle as he laughed again.
She could feel him studying her intently, and
she had to force herself to sit still.

'You tell me.' His voice dropped another

notch and the laughter disappeared. 'Why did you run away?'

Really? Here and now? Because she was so not going into it here.

'I didn't—'

'Laura Kemp?'

Saved. Bless James and his timing. She leapt to her feet.

'Good luck.'

He really didn't mean it, either. He was only being polite, just as she'd been, but she thanked him anyway and walked towards James, her legs oddly wobbly and James's smile of encouragement not really working, because he was only part of a panel and they had to go for the best person for the job.

Had to. And it wouldn't be her. Not in a million years, not with Tom in the line-up, but she wasn't going down without a fight. No way. If he got this job over her, it was going to be because he'd earned it, not because she'd given it away.

She straightened her spine, pinned on her best game face and walked into the interview with her head held high.

* * *

Tom watched the door close behind her and blew out a long, silent breath, feeling the tension drain out of him.

Of all the people to run into, and of all the times, just when his life had fallen apart and he was looking for a fresh start. The last thing he needed was that kind of distraction—although judging by the way she'd reacted to him, it seemed highly unlikely that she'd want to turn back the clock to a relationship that had never even got past first base.

She was right, it was awkward. Very awkward, not only because of the job, but because of the way they'd left it.

Or rather, she'd left it.

He'd asked her out so many times, and every time she'd laughed at him and brushed him aside with a joke at his expense, so he hadn't really believed it when she'd gone with him to the Leavers' Ball. It was his last opportunity to get her to change her mind about him before they all went their separate ways and he lost her for ever, and it had felt like the start of something real between them, something genuine and heartfelt.

They'd danced all night, the tension between them winding tighter and tighter with every brush of their bodies, and at the end he'd asked her to go home with him. He'd been stunned when she'd said yes, and then at the last minute she'd changed her mind and called a taxi, so he'd gone back to his flat to nurse his battered ego and try to work out why. What had he done wrong?

Nothing, probably, and it was a woman's prerogative to change her mind, but she hadn't given him any clues, so he still didn't know why. He didn't know why it mattered so much, either, but apparently it did, and seeing her again had done nothing but stir it up all over again.

He could have asked her at the time, but he hadn't tried to contact her. That would have looked desperate and there was no way he'd been going there, so he'd decided to wait and see how she played it the next time they ran into each other.

Only they never had because she'd gone home the next day without even saying goodbye.

And that was it. No more Laura, taunting

him from afar with her quiet ways and refusal to play. No more jokey put-downs, no more bumping into her in the library—nothing. He hadn't seen her again until today, and it had awakened all sorts of not very comfortable memories.

Where had she been? What had she done for the past seven years? And why on earth was she locuming? That didn't sound like much of a gap year, so why had she needed a break?

Not that he could talk. He'd ditched his job in London and was walking away from his entire life without a backward glance after it had all gone wrong. Maybe she'd felt the same?

None of your business.

He hauled in a breath and stood up. He didn't need to wait there. He'd been asked to come back at two thirty for the second round of interviews, and it was only eleven now. He could go for a wander, take a look around the seaside town, see what he thought of it. He'd never been to Yoxburgh before. It could be interesting to see what his future home might be like.

The interview was as awful as she'd expected. They asked her all the usual horrible questions that relied on bigging herself up, not something she was fond of, and interrogated her on a million clinical and ethical aspects of her role that she was more comfortable with, but it was gruelling and she was just glad when it was over. Well, until this afternoon when she had to do it all over again, apparently, but at least she'd got through to the second round. Like Tom.

He seemed to have disappeared, to her relief, so she didn't have to face him again for the next three hours. She'd have time to take Millie for a nice walk on the cliff top, then back home for lunch before it all kicked off again this afternoon. Maybe by then she'd get her composure back.

She let herself in and Millie was there to greet her, wafting her tail and smiling in the way that only Golden Retrievers seem to do, and she felt her angst melt away.

'Hello, sweetheart,' she said softly, reaching down and smoothing the soft, silky head that pressed into her hand. She started to lean and Laura stepped away.

'Not on my interview trousers. I know you

and your hair. I need to change, OK? Then we can have a cuddle.'

Millie followed her into the bedroom and hopped on the bed, flopping down with a huge sigh with her head on her paws and watching patiently as Laura stripped off her clothes, pulled on jeans and a thick sweater and headed for the door again.

'Come on, then. Let's go.'

Millie leapt off the bed and shot past, her tail waving like a plume as she waited at the door for Laura to join her, the lead in her mouth at the ready. Laura clipped it on and they set off, with Millie walking beautifully by her side.

She'd been the best guide dog, the kindest, sweetest friend, the dearest companion to her grandfather, and now to her. She was so glad she'd been allowed to keep her, because there'd been days when Millie was the only thing that had got her out of bed, the only thing worth living for, and she didn't know what would happen to them if Tom got the post and she ended up with nothing.

She couldn't stay here without a job, so she'd either have to let the house or sell it. Either possibility broke her heart, for Millie as much as for herself. It was their home, the only real home she'd ever known, the only link either of them had to her grandfather. And whatever she ended up doing, wherever they went, she'd have to clear the house of all his possessions.

Starting with ten thousand books, at the last count, but there were probably more by now. Not that he'd been able to read for years, even with a magnifying glass and a light. He'd known each book, though. Where it was, what was in it. And sometimes she'd had to thumb through a book to remind him of something— a quote, some remote fact, the answer to one of her endless questions.

Oh, how she missed him. That brilliant mind, the quiet humour, the gentleness as he'd guided her through the rocky teenage years into adulthood while her mother ricocheted through life like a stray bullet, damaging everyone in her path—

Millie suddenly swung across and blocked her legs as a car shot out of a driveway in front of her. She hadn't heard or seen it, hadn't even been aware of her surroundings, but Millie had, and by snapping back into guide dog mode, she'd probably saved her life.

'You're such a good girl,' she said softly, reaching down to touch the warm, sensible head with a suddenly shaky hand. She sniffed and scrubbed the tears off her cheeks, and straightened up. 'Come on, then. Let's go.'

Millie trotted along beside her, then sat at the kerb, and as they crossed to the other side she saw Tom walking towards them, absolutely the last person she wanted to see while she was having a wobble, but there was no polite way to avoid him and anyway, he'd already spotted them.

'Hi, there,' he murmured, then looked down, a smile softening his face. 'Well, look at you, aren't you just the most gorgeous thing?'

He held a hand out for Millie to sniff, her tail waving in a friendly greeting as he bent and tickled her chest, prompting her to lean firmly against his dark suit trousers. Oops.

'So what's your name, pretty lady?'

'Millie. She was my grandfather's dog.'

He straightened up slowly and searched her eyes, his steady gaze thoughtful. 'Was?' he asked softly after a moment, and she realised what she'd said.

'Is…' And then, because she didn't lie and it was a bit late to be economical with the truth, she let out a quiet breath and went on, 'Was. He died four months ago, at the end of October. He had a stroke last March, then another, and he just faded away. That's what I meant by OK, because he hated it and now it's over and he's at peace.'

His eyes creased in sympathy. 'Oh, Laura. That's tough.'

Nothing else, to her relief; no platitudes, nothing about a blessed release or how was she coping or any of the other things she didn't want to hear.

She nodded. 'It is. But we're getting there, aren't we, Millie?' She turned her attention to the dog, anything rather than look any longer into those sympathetic, beautiful eyes. She didn't want his sympathy. Didn't want anything from him. What was he even doing here in Yoxburgh? He was a party animal! There were no wild parties in Yoxburgh, just the odd beach barbecue. Unless he knew something she didn't.

The silence hung in the air between them,

and she finally broke it. 'I need to take Millie for a run on the cliff top. I'll see you later. Millie, let's go.'

It was a clear dismissal, but he ignored it, because he'd seen the grief in her eyes, still raw, and he knew how much her grandfather had meant to her. Maybe she needed to talk. It wouldn't be the first time.

'Can I tag along? I haven't got as far as the sea yet.'

He fell into step beside her without waiting for her consent, but her shoulders stiffened, making him frown and reconsider.

She didn't want him there.

Really, really didn't want him there, and he didn't want to make it any more awkward than it already was. He pulled out his phone, pretended to find a message and stopped walking.

'Actually, sorry, I'm going to have to pass, I've got to deal with this. I'll see you later at the hospital.'

'OK.'

She sounded relieved, and he watched her go, but she didn't so much as glance back. She let the dog off when she reached the grass verge on the other side of the road, throwing a ball for Millie over and over again until she lost interest, then walking on and heading down some steps out of sight.

He slid the phone back into his pocket and stared after her, feeling oddly unsettled.

He'd thought the awkwardness was about the way they'd parted, but maybe it wasn't. Maybe it wasn't that she felt guilty—after all, what did she really have to feel guilty for? It wasn't like she'd dumped him at the altar. Maybe it really was all about the job, the job she desperately needed to get her life back on track, and he was a threat to that, a very real threat in many ways.

Her childhood home was here, in Yoxburgh. Not only that, but judging by the familiar way James Slater had greeted her, she'd presumably been doing locum work in Yoxburgh Park Hospital so she could care for her grandfather after his stroke. No wonder she'd applied for the job. It must have felt made for her, hugely important to her future and security, and if he got it he'd take that away from her, so of course she didn't want him there, with so much riding on it.

There wasn't another hospital for miles, so if she didn't get it she'd have to move away, and it could break her heart to leave. From what he remembered this was the only real home she'd ever known, and now he was here, rocking up out of nowhere to steal her job from under her and threaten her security.

Should he withdraw, find something else?

No. That was ridiculous. They might not even offer it to him, and if they offered it to someone else, they wouldn't turn it down because of her. Why would they? That was crazy—and anyway, he wanted it. Needed it, every bit as much as she did. More, maybe.

He had to get out of London, away from everything that had happened, somewhere where the pace of life was slower and he could draw breath after a hideous year that had done its best to break him, both personally and professionally.

But what if he got it and it turned her life upside down? He could get a job anywhere. They were crying out for people like him, and he had no ties anywhere else, not any more. He could find somewhere else that was still reasonably near his family in Cambridge, but this place was all she had. He should withdraw, give her a better chance—

He gave a hollow laugh. That was a massive assumption. There was always the possibility she'd get the job over him, especially if she had been locuming there in the hospital. That would surely give her a head start, although they seemed to have quite a large field for the interviews. But James had definitely smiled at her very warmly, so it clearly wasn't going to be a walk-over, even though he'd felt his interview had gone well.

Whatever. One more session to get through and he'd have his answer, and maybe he'd get a chance afterwards to talk to Laura. They'd been good friends, although he'd always wanted it to be more than that, and it would be good to mend fences.

He wished he knew why she'd changed her mind that night. Had he offended her in some way? In which case maybe he owed her an apology. He didn't think she'd just got cold feet. She'd seemed every bit as keen as he was, and she'd been all over him while they were dancing. Unless she'd just been stringing him along for kicks, meaning to walk off all along?

No, that wasn't Laura, not the Laura he knew, and it certainly wasn't the way she'd kissed him back, either, but he still wanted to know why she'd walked away, and seven years didn't seem to have made a scrap of difference to that.

They'd whittled it down to three candidates by the afternoon session: her; Steve, the fidgety, bored one; and Tom.

Of course Tom. That had always been a given.

Had she done all right? She wasn't sure, but Tom would have aced it. She didn't know about Steve, but he didn't look any too happy.

Then, when they were all done, they were brought tea and biscuits, and after a while Steve was called in and left with a rueful wave to them. Then James came out with a wry smile.

'Well, you two have given us a bit of a problem. In an ideal world we'd take you both on, but it isn't an ideal world so, hard as it is, we have to make a decision and at the moment it's too close to call. Is there any possibility you could come back tomorrow morning at ten to give us more time?'

Seriously?

'Sure,' she said, her nerves jangling, and out of the corner of her eye she saw Tom nod, his spontaneous smile at the ready.

'Of course. No problem.'

'Good. We'll see you both here at ten tomorrow, then. Thank you.'

James went back into the meeting room and closed the door, and she stared at it, wondering how much longer it could possibly be before they put her out of her misery.

'How long can they drag it out, for heaven's sake?' she said with a grumpy sigh, and he chuckled.

'Who knows?' he murmured, then looked at her thoughtfully. 'Fancy a cup of tea?'

No. And anyway, the last thing she needed was to spend any more time in Tom's company. 'We just had one.'

He smiled wryly. 'So we did. How about a drink, then?'

'A drink?' she said, slightly stunned that he should even suggest it. 'It's a bit early.'

He raised an eyebrow and smiled again. 'I meant later. We could catch up.'

Or talk about that night, which was hanging around like the elephant in the room. She looked away from those piercingly intense dark eyes, cross with herself for the pang of guilt she felt. *Still* felt. 'Maybe I don't want to talk about it?'

'Talk about what?'

His voice was all innocence, and she rolled her eyes and gave a short sigh and he shrugged and smiled, his mouth hitching up in a way that made her heart thud.

'OK, we don't have to talk about that, but I have to go back to my hotel and check in again for another night, and then I'll have the evening to kill. You could have dinner with me for old times' sake?'

She stared at him wide-eyed. 'Old times' sake?'

'Why not? I've missed you and your acerbic tongue.'

'I don't have—'

'Oh, you do. I've still got the scars.' His mouth tipped into a rueful smile, the sort that could unravel her in a heartbeat. 'Come on. I promise I won't raise the subject.'

She wasn't sure she believed him, but she could feel herself weakening, just as she'd always weakened, but only to a point. And he was right, they had been friends and it would be churlish to refuse.

'OK, but later. I need to go home and change, and Millie will need to be fed and walked, so I can't come for a while.'

'Let's make it seven, then.' He told her the hotel's name and address, and she nodded.

'I know where it is. I'll see you in Reception.'

'Make it the bar. That way I won't look ridiculous when you don't rock up because you've changed your mind.'

And he talked about *her* acerbic tongue?

He walked away with a cocky grin leaving her fuming at his little dig, and the door of the meeting room opened again and James came out.

'Laura. Were you waiting to see me?'

'No, Tom was talking to me but he's just left.'

Right before I killed him...

James nodded thoughtfully. 'Yes, I guessed from your CVs that you'd know each other.'

'Well, we did, but I haven't seen him since uni.' They'd even been housemates for a couple of years in the middle, but she wasn't telling James that in case he got the wrong end of the stick. It was messy enough as it was.

James nodded again, then sighed. 'Look, I'm really sorry about this, I hate protracting it but it's not what I expected. Tom was a late applicant, and—well, he's good. As good as you. We can't ignore that.'

Of course they couldn't. 'Look, James, it's OK,' she lied. 'I know you have to be absolutely sure.'

'We are sure. We're sure you're both excellent candidates, in your different ways. That's why it's so hard.'

'You could always just toss a coin.'

He smiled and shook his head ruefully. 'Don't joke about it, it's been suggested, but no. I just wish we could have you both, because your skills and experience would complement each other, but...'

'But you can't. I know that. You don't have the luxury of unlimited funding. It's OK,

James, I understand. Do what you have to do and don't worry about me. I'll be all right whatever happens. We both will. There are plenty of other jobs out there. I'll see you tomorrow morning.'

He nodded and she turned away, heading for the lift down to the ground floor. She had to get back to Millie, especially if she was going out again in two hours. Not that she wanted to. Just the thought of spending time alone with him made her edgy, but he'd promised he wasn't going to raise the subject of that night.

Did she believe him? Probably not, but he was right, they had been friends, and she did owe him an apology for the way she'd left it.

Even if he was about to steal the job she'd hoped was hers and trash the future she'd dared to dream of…

CHAPTER TWO

SHE WAS LATE.

Only a few minutes, but it was enough to make him wonder if she'd just been stringing him along. Like she had before? Dammit, if he'd fallen for it again—no, she was probably only doing it for the hell of it, just because of what he'd said. That would teach him to make wisecracks.

He was on the point of leaving when she walked in, looking slightly harassed and a little wary, and he felt the tension drain away like water through a sieve. He slid off the bar stool and walked towards her with a smile.

Her answering smile looked rather like relief, as if she hadn't expected him to be there either.

'Hi. Sorry I'm late. I got held up and I didn't have your number so I couldn't call you.'

'I thought you'd bottled.'

She raised an eyebrow. 'Well, I didn't, which

is more than you deserve, so don't push your luck. I'm here now.'

And he was ridiculously pleased about that. Without engaging his brain, he dropped a kiss on her cheek, and the familiar scent of her perfume hit him in the midsection like a stray rocket, robbing him of breath.

Why on earth had he thought this was a good idea?

Why did he have to do that? And how could it still have such a crazy effect on her? Hadn't she moved on at all in seven years?

'So what held you up? Or *were* you just teaching me a lesson?' he asked with a wry twist to his lips.

'I'm not that petty—not that you didn't deserve it after that parting shot,' she said, trying to sound scathing while her heart was pumping furiously. 'It was Millie. She was a bit funny about me going out again. I think she thought I was going to be on night duty and she struggles with that after all she's been through.'

'We can always go back to yours if you don't want to leave her,' he offered, but there was no way they were doing that, not with her heart leaping about every time he smiled at her, which he seemed to be doing rather a lot.

She shook her head. 'Don't worry about it. I'm sure she'll be fine. She needs to get used to it.'

'So what can I get you to drink?'

Not alcohol. She certainly didn't need that, and anyway, she was driving. 'Sparkling water?'

He ordered it and scanned the room, while she wished her heart would settle down and be just a little less happy to see him. This was such a bad idea...

'Do you want to sit in here for a bit, or would you rather eat now? There's a table over there.'

She turned around and spotted a spare table tucked away in a corner near the window. She hadn't eaten, but there was a knot of tension sitting like a ball of lead in her stomach. Still, he'd promised not to talk about that night— although at least that might stop her fantasising over the feel of his lips against her cheek...

'Here for now, and then maybe eat in a little while?' she said, her voice irritatingly breathless still, and headed across the room. It was only after she'd shrugged off her coat and sat down that she realised what an intimate feel the little table gave them in its cosy, quiet corner. Why, oh, why was she here?

He brought their drinks over and sat down opposite her, and she picked up her glass and looked up at him. Not a good move. His eyes, always so eloquent, were unnervingly silent. Her mouth felt dry, and she took a gulp of fizzy water, her heart pounding even harder. They should have stayed at the bar. At least that way she wouldn't have had to look at him.

Please say something. Stop looking at me like that with those mesmerising eyes.

He broke the silence first, his voice a low murmur as he cut straight to the point without a single nicety, his searching gaze holding her eyes against her will.

'What did I do wrong, Laura? Why did you go?'

Her heart slammed against her ribs, and she looked away.

'I thought we weren't going to talk about this?'

'Yeah, we weren't, but—it's bugged me for years. I just want to understand. Did I say something to upset you? Do something? Or was it just to cut me down to size?'

'No! Not at all. I wouldn't do that. You know me better than that.'

'So what, then?'

She shrugged. 'I just realised that sleeping with you at that stage was all wrong. It was only one night. What was the point of that?'

'Who said anything about one night?'

She nearly laughed at that. 'What else could it have been, Tom? A week, max? We were going to different parts of the country, with no future, no prospect of a relationship. How was that supposed to work? It was doomed to failure.'

'So why say yes in the first place? Why not just say no and have done with it? You'd had plenty of practice. It wouldn't have been the first time you'd told me to take a hike.'

No, it wouldn't, and that was why she'd moved back into halls at the start of the final year, because she could feel herself weakening. And then he'd left it to the last minute to launch his final charm offensive, and she'd fallen for it.

She shrugged. 'Call it a moment of weakness. Then it dawned on me it was just because it was your last chance before we all left, a final pop at breaking down my defences. And you always rise to a challenge. That's why you'll get this job. You weren't really interested in me, Tom, you know that. I was just the last box that needed ticking.'

He looked astonished, and she felt a flicker of doubt.

'That's rubbish. Of course I was interested in you.'

'No, you weren't. I'm not your type. You like tall, leggy blondes.'

'You're a blonde.'

'Not in the right way, and I'll never be leggy. Why would you want a dull and boring little academic when you could have any one of the party girls?'

He frowned, his eyes puzzled. 'You're not dull and boring.'

'I was compared to them. You could have had anyone there you wanted, and let's face it, they *all* wanted you. They couldn't understand why you kept asking me, and why on earth I should say no. I think they thought I should be flattered.'

'Flattered?'

'Absolutely.'

His eyes narrowed thoughtfully. 'Is that why you ran out on me? Because you thought it was just flattery?'

'Pretty much. And anyway, I didn't run—'

'You did. I thought you'd changed your mind about me at last, and then you slammed on the brakes, told me you didn't want to talk about it and ran away, and it was so unlike you. You'd never done that before, you'd always told me firmly where to go. It was just so out of character.'

'Maybe you didn't know me as well as you think you did. And I didn't run, I walked, because I came to my senses, and I'm glad I did because otherwise I would have been so mad with myself for falling for all the nonsense.'

He shook his head. 'It wasn't nonsense. I meant it.'

'What, all that rubbish about me being sexy and beautiful? Come on, Tom. I'm not that gullible.'

'It wasn't rubbish—'

'Yes, it was. You knew I'd fall for it, and you couldn't bear to be rejected because that would mean you'd lost, and you're hard wired to win, even if you have to lie to do it.'

He shook his head in disbelief.

'Oh, come on, that's unfair, I've never lied to you, and whatever else you might be, you've never been unfair. Distant, yes, and standoffish, but unfair? No. It's just not you. You're better than that.'

She read the sincerity in his eyes, and swallowed hard, feeling a little guilty but also stung by his words.

'Am I distant? Standoffish?'

'You can be. You have a very good putdown. I should know, you used it on me often enough.'

He was smiling now, but it was a little twisted and he sounded hurt. Odd, that. He always used to laugh it off. His come-ons were always jokey—weren't they? But there was a vulnerability in his eyes she'd never seen before.

'You didn't give up, though,' she said slowly, wondering why not. Had he honestly thought she was sexy and beautiful?

He smiled wryly. 'No, I didn't,' he murmured, the smile fading after a moment. 'You really believed it, didn't you? That I was just saying it to get you into bed?'

'Of course I did—it was a means to an end, the end being me in this case, but I didn't want to be another notch on your bedpost. I'm worth more than that, and it wasn't like you needed any more,' she said, watching him wince, and then went on, 'and anyway, you know the old saying about never belonging to a club that'll have you as a member.'

'There was no club!'

'Oh, yes, there was, Tom. Of course there was, and all the girls wanted to be in it. And I realised that I didn't want to belong to it, because that would make me just the same as them, and I didn't want to be like them.'

'You could never be like them. It's was one of the things I liked most about you. And anyway, for the record, you're not dull and boring, you're a grafter.'

'It's the same thing.'

'No, it's not. So what made you go? Because the next day I found out you'd left, and I didn't even get a chance to say goodbye.'

She looked down, feeling a little guilty about that if nothing else. 'I know. I'm sorry. I went back to halls, and I realised I just couldn't face you again, so I packed my stuff and drove back to Suffolk as soon as it was light.'

He shook his head again with what looked like regret.

'I wish you'd talked to me, Laura,' he said softly.

'I couldn't. I knew you'd talk me round if I gave you half a chance. It was easier to run away. And you were right about that, too. I did run, metaphorically speaking, but at least I did it with my head held high and nothing to be ashamed of.'

He met her eyes, his filled again with something she couldn't quite read. Hurt, maybe, and that vulnerability again.

'Is that what sleeping with me would have been? Something to be ashamed of?'

She looked away. 'Not because of you. Because of what it would say about me. I didn't want to be like my mother.'

'Your *mother*?'

'Yes, my mother. She'd sleep with anyone who'd have her. She would have been in your club without a doubt, given the chance.'

'Wow'' She felt his fingers curl around her

hand as it lay on the table, the warm pressure as he squeezed it gently. 'I'm sorry, that's... But, you know, being with me wouldn't have made you the same as her. Not that I know anything about her, but I know you, and you have a right to a life, Laura, to make your own choices. You would have had nothing to be ashamed of.'

'But I would have been.'

He shook his head sadly. 'I wish you'd told me how you felt, talked about it then, instead of leaving without a word.'

So did she, but she hadn't, and it was done now. Been done for seven years...

When she didn't answer he let go of her hand and sat back, leaving her fingers cold and lonely on the table. She curled them into her palm and dropped her hand into her lap, trying to stifle the tingle of longing left by his touch, but it didn't work.

'Speak to me,' he said softly, and she made herself look up and meet his eyes, warm and sincere and, yes, a little hurt, and she felt another pang of guilt.

'I'm sorry,' she said with a wash of remorse. 'I honestly didn't mean to hurt you. It didn't occur to me for a moment that you'd really care, but I still shouldn't have left it like that. I should have explained, but I knew you'd talk me round and I didn't want that. You're a heartbreaker, Tom, and I didn't want my heart broken, but you're right, I owed you more than that. You deserved better, and at the very least I should have said goodbye.'

His smile was touched with sadness. 'Yes, you should. I would have listened, would have understood. Still, it's all water under the bridge now. I'm sure we've both moved on.'

He held her eyes for a long moment, then hauled in a breath and glanced at his watch. 'It's eight o'clock. I suppose we ought to think about food. Do you want to eat here, or go and find somewhere else?'

The abrupt change of subject made her blink, but she felt her stomach rumble and realised she was hungry. And it might be good to catch up with what he'd been doing and where, and put all this behind them. She smiled at him.

'There's a decent Thai restaurant down on the sea front. Want to give it a go? We can walk, it's not far.'

'Yeah, why not? That sounds nice.'

* * *

It was nice.

Rather too nice, in fact. She'd forgotten how funny he was, how well they'd got on when he wasn't trying to convince her to go to bed with him.

They walked along the prom, listening to the sound of the waves lapping against the sea defences as they made their way to the little restaurant, the brisk February wind making them hurry.

They shared several dishes, fighting over the last tiger prawn, and she lost—only she didn't, because he speared it and held it out to her, leaning over the table and holding it to her lips.

She opened her mouth and took it, and it seemed suddenly shockingly intimate, shockingly sensual and—her body was rioting, her eyes locked on his, and all the sensible reasons why she shouldn't touch him with a barge pole flew out of the window.

Then he broke the searing eye contact and put his fork down.

'Right, I think we're done,' he said, his voice sounding a little odd as he pushed his plate away and attracted the waitress's attention. 'Can we have the bill, please?'

'I'll pay—'

'No, you won't. This was my idea. You can pay next time.'

'What, in seven years?' she said, and he laughed and looked away at the card machine, leaving her breathless with longing and wishing she hadn't chickened out that night, and then she might not have spent the last seven years telling herself she'd done the right thing and regretting her missed opportunity.

'Right, let's go.'

He got to his feet, smiled at the waitress and held Laura's coat for her as she put it on, his hands settling it gently round her shoulders, lifting her hair free with warm, careful fingers that left little rivers of fire in their wake. He shrugged into his jacket, opened the door for her and they walked back up towards his hotel.

And then he tripped on the kerb as they crossed the road, and grabbed her arm.

'Whoa! You OK?'

'Yeah, I'm fine.' He straightened up and shook his head. 'Sorry. I just didn't see that.'

'Are you going blind, or was that just an excuse to grab me?' she teased, and then wondered why she'd opened her mouth because she could suddenly feel the tension between them zinging in the cold night air.

'Rumbled,' he said lightly, and dropped her arm as if it was red hot. He set off again without another word, but she could feel the imprint of his fingers on her arm all the way back to the hotel, warm and tingling.

'Did you walk or drive?' he said as they reached the entrance to the car park.

'I drove, because I was already late. My car's just here.'

They paused beside it, his face shadowed by the light above him so she couldn't read his eyes, but the zing was still there.

'D'you fancy a coffee?' he asked, his voice low. 'The bar's still open.'

Coffee? Coffee wasn't even on her radar, and she was pretty sure it wasn't on his, either, but still she hesitated for longer than she should have.

'No, I—I'd better go. Millie. But thank you for a lovely dinner. It was good to catch up— to sort things out.'

'It was. Although I wish we'd done it seven years ago.'

'What, and given you a chance to talk me round? No way.'

He gave a soft huff of laughter, and shook his head, his expression wry. 'You don't give up, do you?'

'You can talk.'

She hesitated for a second, then, ignoring the little voice of warning squealing in the background, she went up on tiptoe and brushed a kiss against his cheek, the soft rasp of stubble against her lips lighting more fires that raced through her veins. She dropped back onto her heels and took a tiny step back.

'I need to go,' she said, her voice oddly breathless.

He nodded. 'Probably wise.'

And then he paused, his lips pursing thoughtfully before he spoke again, his voice low and somehow sad. 'I'm sorry, Laura.'

'What about? Just being you?'

'No. The job thing. I should pull out—'

'No! No, Tom, you shouldn't. And anyway, there's nothing to say they'll give it to you,' she added with a teasing smile. 'Maybe they'll give it to me. Miracles have been known to happen. And I certainly don't need the condescension of your grand gestures. I'm quite employable, you know.'

It was meant as a joke, and she was relieved when his mouth tipped into a crooked smile. 'Well, that would be poetic justice. Teach me to be so arrogant. Perhaps I *should* have been apologising for being me.'

She felt another pang of guilt, but before she could speak he bent his head and touched his lips lightly to hers, then straightened up, leaving her mouth tingling. 'I'll see you tomorrow at ten.'

'We could meet for coffee before,' she said, suddenly realising that it might be their last chance to spend time together and surprised that she didn't want that to happen.

'Make it breakfast. Nine?'

'OK. The Park Café near the ED is nice. We could meet there?'

'Sure. I'll see you tomorrow.'

She nodded, telling herself she ought to go before she could do anything rash like kiss him again, but for some reason she hesitated, her heart suddenly starting to pound as their eyes locked in the semi-darkness, her breath catching as everything seemed to go into slow motion.

His breath drifted over her skin, making her nerve endings dance, and his hand came up and touched her face, his fingers gentle as he stared down at her with those dark eyes. She still couldn't read them, but she could read the hitch in his breath, the tension in his body as his arms slid round her, and she sank against the solid warmth of his chest and lifted her mouth to his.

He'd forgotten.

Forgotten how it had felt to kiss her, how eager and filled with longing her mouth had been, how much he'd wanted her, and as he pulled her closer and deepened the kiss, he felt the years roll away, the sense of loss, regret, disappointment all fading away and taking them right back to that last night, when they'd come so close...

He couldn't let her go—not now, when fate had given them one last chance.

'Stay with me,' he murmured, kissing her, nibbling her lips, brushing his mouth back and forth against hers and feeling the soft drag of their damp lips clinging.

She eased away, doubt in her eyes—doubt, and a longing he'd never really seen before. Maybe never been allowed to see. Or maybe in the darkness he was just seeing what he wanted to see...

He cradled her cheek in his hand, his heart pounding. 'Stay with me,' he said again, clearly this time, his voice soft and coaxing and a little gruff because he wanted her *so much*.

'I...'

He held his breath, his fingers threading gently through her hair, sifting it, waiting. He felt as much as saw the moment she crumbled, the moment common sense flew out of the window, and she tilted her head back and met his eyes.

And then she nodded, just the tiniest movement, and he felt the breath leave him in a rush. He wrapped his arms around her and held her for a moment, then turned and led her back into the hotel, picked up his key and walked with her to his room in a silence taut with promise.

He fumbled the key card and had to try

again, and then they were in, the door closed behind them, and the only sound in the room was their ragged breathing.

He lifted a hand and touched her face, reading her eyes in a way he'd not really been able to in the dim light of the car park.

Want, need—and still a trace of uncertainty? He didn't want to see that. Didn't want her to feel she'd been pressured to do something she'd later regret. Above all he didn't want her to feel ashamed, of all things.

'Are you sure about this? I don't want you doing anything you're not happy with, anything that's going to make you feel bad about yourself.'

And it was gone. The uncertainty, the hesitation, the doubt, gone from her eyes in an instant with those few words, and he felt the breath leave him in a silent rush.

Was she certain? No. Was she bottling out this time? Also no. She'd waited far too long already and she wanted an end to the nagging ache of longing that had plagued her for years.

She took a step back from him, shrugged off her coat and dropped it over the back of a chair. Her boots followed, then the baby-soft jumper the same blue as her eyes, peeled slowly over her head.

'Well, are you going to stand there like a voyeur, or are you going to join me?'

He let out a strangled laugh and ditched his coat, then caught her hands as she reached for her jeans.

'Wait,' he said gruffly. 'I want to do that.'

But not yet, apparently, because he heeled off his shoes, tugged his shirt over his head and reached for his belt.

'Wait. I want to do that,' she echoed.

He stopped, his mouth quirking, one eyebrow raised over eyes the colour of a dark winter sea, the storm still raging in them even though he was still.

She laid a hand over his heart, felt the skin like hot silk beneath her fingertips, the soft brush of hair against her palm over the heavy pounding of his heart. She could feel its echo in her throat, hear it in her ears, the want, the need. Her hand moved down, feeling his muscles tighten beneath her fingers, pulling the end of the belt out of the loops, tugging it back to release the prong from the leather, sliding it free so she could reach the stud.

'Wait.'

He stepped back and slid his hands into his pockets, pulled out his wallet, keys, a handful of coins which he dumped on the bedside table. He turned the bedside lights on low, cut the overhead light and then held out his hand to her.

'Come here.'

Heart thrashing, she took a step towards him, mesmerised by the storm of need raging in his eyes.

So much need. And it definitely wasn't flattery, because his pupils were dilated, his breathing fast and tight, his focus absolute. He wanted her. He really, really wanted her.

She felt his hands on her waist, hooking into the top of her jeans and peeling them down, down, over her legs, and she could hardly breathe. She wiggled her feet free, socks and all, and straightened up in just her underwear, and he swore softly under his breath and reached for his own jeans.

'Uh-uh. Mine.'

She slapped his hands away lightly, and he

gave her a smile that was mostly grimace and dropped his hands. She slid her fingers inside his waistband, feeling the tantalising brush of hair against her hand, and his abdomen went as taut as a drum, the breath hissing out of his mouth as the zip slid down.

She hesitated, a sudden wave of doubt sweeping over her. Was she crazy? How would she feel tomorrow? Not ashamed, not now, because this was on her terms and as he'd said, she had a right to a life, but was she just setting herself up for heartache?

She felt his knuckles graze her cheek.

'Hey.'

She looked up and met his eyes, and saw reassurance.

'It's OK. You can still change your mind if you want,' he said softly, and she blinked.

No way. It wasn't that, more the fact that once done, this could never be undone and she wasn't sure she'd be strong enough to lose him once she'd let him that close.

But there was nothing *to* lose. She didn't have him, never had had, and there was no future for them. This was just a one-off, their farewell, closure on their unfinished business.

Her last chance. And this time she was going to take it.

'I do want to. We've waited a long time for this. Let's not wait any longer.'

She laid a hand against his jaw and felt it clench, felt the movement in his throat as he swallowed.

And then he nodded, and a gentle smile touched his lips. 'OK. But let's take it slow. I've waited seven years for this, I want to do it justice.'

His eyes were serious, curiously intent, and he let go of her hand and threaded his fingers through her hair, his mouth finding hers again, slowly building the tension until she wanted to scream.

He moved on, his mouth teasing, tormenting, over her jaw, the side of her neck, then lower, down over her collar bones, pausing at the little hollow between them, then on, his tongue lazily tracing the edge of her bra over her thrashing heart.

'We've got too much on,' he muttered, and kicked off his jeans, shucked off his shorts and socks and then gently peeled away her underwear. Then he stood back and looked at her, shaking his head slowly from side to side as his eyes raked her body hungrily.

'You are beautiful, you know. Beautiful and as sexy as hell. Do you have the slightest idea how much I want you?'

His voice was gruff, hoarse with emotion, and she felt her knees buckle. Definitely not flattery.

He pulled her slowly up against him, sucking in his breath as their skin came into contact from top to toe, and his mouth found hers again, urgent now, touched with desperation.

Was hers? Probably. If it wasn't she had no idea why because she was desperate now, desperate for the feel of his body on hers, in hers.

His hands were all over her, deft and clever, and then suddenly they were gone, and he was throwing back the bedclothes and reaching for her again.

They fell onto the mattress in a tangle of legs and roaming hands, his body taut and hot against hers, one leg nudging hers apart as they rocked against each other. Then he paused and groped for his wallet, swearing softly under his breath as he fumbled with the little foil packet.

She took the task out of his hands, dragging a shuddering groan from low down in his chest, and then she was back in his arms, skin to skin, heart to heart, their bodies merging into one, engulfed in a fireball of need and tenderness and sensory overload like nothing she'd ever known before.

He held her as it ripped through them, his body stiffening and then sagging in her arms as the tension drained out of them, leaving them spent and breathless.

And when the last flickers had died away and their breathing had slowed, he turned down the light, pulled the covers over them and cradled her wordlessly in his arms, one hand stroking her back with a gentleness that unravelled her. She could hear the slow, steady beat of his heart under her ear, feel the rise and fall of his chest as he breathed in and out, the slackening of tension in his muscles as he slid into sleep and his hand went still.

She felt her eyelids drooping, felt her body sinking into oblivion, then reality wrenched her awake.

Millie.

Poor Millie. She'd forgotten her—forgotten

everything, in the storm of white heat and tenderness that had engulfed them—and the last thing she wanted was to leave, because she knew this would be the last time she saw him alone, the last time he'd hold her. But she had no choice. She had to put Millie first.

She feathered a gentle kiss against his cheek. 'Tom, I have to go. I can't leave Millie.'

'Mmm.'

Had he really heard? She wasn't sure, but she eased out from under his arm, wriggled off the bed and pulled on her clothes, glad he'd left the light on low so she could find them. Should she leave him a note? Maybe, but she didn't have a pen or paper.

Should she wake him?

No. He'd only talk her into staying longer, and the poor dog was waiting. Time to get back to reality.

She laid a gentle kiss on his cheek, picked up her coat and with a last regretful backward glance she let herself out.

He woke to silence.

Silence, darkness, and a cold, empty space beside him. Levering himself up on one elbow, he turned up the light and scanned the room, but all trace of her was gone, leaving nothing behind but memories and the lingering scent of her perfume on the sheets.

Why had she left? Had she said anything to him? He didn't think so...

He let out a sigh. Millie. Of course.

He flopped back onto the mattress and stared at the ceiling, his mind filled with images of her body, the taste of her still in his mouth.

She'd been amazing. Incredible. He'd never felt so connected, so involved, so deeply certain of what he was doing. Not now, though. Now, she was gone, and reality slapped him firmly in the face.

They were going nowhere. Or at least, not together. One of them was going to get the job, and the other would be who knows where.

Would he be the one to get it? He hoped so, even though it would mean that Laura didn't, because this job was far more to him than a means to an end, a leg-up on his career ladder. It was a lifeline, a completely fresh start when the future he'd thought was mapped out in front of him had crumbled into dust.

Not that Karen had had the decency to tell

him she'd already moved on, she'd just left him to find out in the most painful and humiliating way possible.

And now he'd slept with Laura, and stirred up another whole welter of emotions that would have been better left untouched.

It was his own stupid fault. He shouldn't have raised the subject, shouldn't have dragged it all out of the closet where it should rightfully have stayed for ever. He should have let her go when she said she was going, but no, he'd had a better idea and they'd ended up in bed.

He shut his eyes, but he couldn't shut out the images of her body, couldn't shut out his memory of what they'd shared.

Idiot. Oh, well, it was done now, and if nothing else it would be a memory he'd treasure.

He so should have left her alone.

He punched the pillow and rolled onto his side, but sleep eluded him and when he finally dozed off his dreams turned to nightmares. He was running through a forest in pitch blackness, gripped by terror, with someone or something close behind him. He could hear their breathing, feel them clawing at him, and then he tripped and fell headlong—

He woke with a jolt, his heart racing, and swung his legs over the side of the bed, turning up the light and driving back the shadows. Gradually his heart slowed, and he got up and went to the bathroom and stared at himself in the mirror.

His eyes were wide, and he could see lingering traces of the terror he'd felt. Why would he dream that? It had been so real, so terrifying, that he could have been there, could have reached out and touched the trees, could have tripped over those roots—

Like the kerb? Was that why he'd dreamt it? Laura had teased him about not seeing it, but he genuinely hadn't seen it, and that worried him now, thinking about it. It wasn't the first time he'd stumbled in the dark, but he'd blamed it on eye strain, tiredness, working ridiculous hours in artificial light, vitamin A deficiency—it could have been anything, really.

But what if she was she right? What if there *was* something wrong with his eyes—or had he just been distracted? He had no idea.

He went back to bed, turned the light down again and lay there, waiting for his eyes to adjust to the darkness, but they didn't, not for an age, and even then it wasn't great.

He felt his pulse pick up. What if it was something serious? No. It couldn't be. Could it? His mind started scrolling through all the differential diagnoses, all the terrifying scenarios that could mean losing his sight.

No. He was being melodramatic and ridiculous. It was just eye strain. Had to be. He'd get his eyes checked, put his mind at rest.

He groped for his phone. Five-thirty. Early, but not too early, and he knew he wouldn't sleep again. He threw back the covers and headed for the shower.

CHAPTER THREE

HE WASN'T THERE.

She scanned the tables but there was no sign of him.

Would he turn up?

Maybe. Maybe not. After all, she'd run out on him. She asked for a cappuccino, picked up a delicious looking but horribly unhealthy almond croissant and headed for a table by the window, her stomach in knots.

She should have woken him before she'd left, but he'd been so heavily asleep and she'd had to get back to Millie. Would he have realised that, or would he have thought she'd done a runner again?

A shadow fell across her and she looked up, her heart picking up speed at the sight of him.

He was smiling, his eyes warm if a little guarded, and she smiled back, slightly shocked at the wave of relief that deluged her. 'Hi. Did you get lost?'

His mouth twitched. 'Hardly. It's pretty well signposted. I'm sorry I'm late. There was a queue to check out of the hotel.'

'Don't worry about it. I'm sorry I ran out on you last night, I had to get back to Millie.'

'Yeah, I realised that.' He glanced down at the table. 'Have you got everything you need?'

Everything except him—

'Yes, thanks, I'm fine. Sorry, I should have waited for you, but I wasn't sure…'

'…if I'd show?' he finished, and his smile was wry. 'Let me just grab a coffee. I had something to eat earlier at the hotel.'

She followed him with her eyes, seeing beneath the beautifully cut suit to the man beneath, the man who'd set fire to her last night, body and soul.

The real Tom?

She shouldn't have slept with him. Should've gone home when she'd had the chance, and she wouldn't be the emotional mess she was now.

He put his coffee down and slid into the seat opposite her, then met her eyes, his own veiled again so she couldn't read them.

'About last night,' he said, his voice quiet and—heavy?

With regret? Too late, the deed was done and there was nothing either of them could do about it. And anyway, it was irrelevant because after today one of them would be in Yoxburgh and the other one—probably her—wouldn't. What more was there to say? Nothing that he'd want to hear.

'What about it?' she murmured. 'It was what it was—tying up the loose ends. That's all,' she lied, because she didn't want him to think she was going all needy on him.

An eyebrow flickered up a fraction and hovered.

'Closure?'

'I think so.'

No, you don't. You don't think so at all. You'll never have closure, not now...

'OK,' he said after a moment, and she felt a wave of relief. He looked down at his coffee, gave it a stir for no good reason, looked up again with expressionless eyes.

'So—I wonder what today's going to bring.'

'An answer, I hope—finally,' she said, her heart giving a sudden thud of nerves. 'I hope you like Yoxburgh.'

He frowned. 'What makes you think I'll need to?'

'Why wouldn't you?'

He gave a soft huff of laughter, his breath drifting across the table and teasing her skin. 'Because they know you?'

'That won't influence them,' she said, not bothering to deny it because he'd obviously worked it out for himself.

He turned his attention to his coffee, stirring it again. 'I wonder if they realise we know each other?'

'Yes, they do, because of our CVs. James mentioned it yesterday afternoon, after you'd gone. I was about to leave and he came out, and we had a chat.'

'About?'

'The delay. Basically he just apologised for dragging it out. I told him he had to do what he had to do.'

'And may the best man win?'

She laughed, and it sounded hollow to her ears. 'Or woman,' she said, because she hadn't entirely given up hope.

Tom frowned at her, his eyes searching. 'You really want this job, don't you?'

'Of course I do, but I only applied because James told me to, and I haven't got as much experience as you, I've had quite a bit of time out with my grandfather and anyway, you've—you're you. End of. They'll go for you. They'd be mad not to.'

'I don't think it's that simple, or they would have decided yesterday.'

'I know. I have no idea why they're struggling.'

'Because you're good? Because they don't want to lose you?'

'But I'm not as good as you. I have less experience.'

'Laura, don't put yourself down. You've always done it. You shouldn't.'

'I'm not putting myself down, Tom, I'm being a realist. Look, do you want some of this? It's huge.'

She tore a chunk off her croissant and gave it to him, and he bit into it, dropping a little scatter of icing sugar down his suit. He gave a disgusted snort. 'Great. I think this suit's magnetic. Do you have any idea how hard it was to get the dog hair off?'

She laughed and took a bite of her own. 'I can imagine. I have to do it all the time.'

He bit again, those white, even teeth sinking through the soft pastry and making her mouth water.

She hauled her eyes off him and concentrated on her own plate, aware of his every bite, every chew, every swallow. Then he wiped his hands on her paper napkin, dusted himself off and looked up at her, his eyes concerned.

'So what will you do? If they do offer it to me?'

She shrugged, trying not to look as worried as she felt. 'I'll find something. They still need locum cover until you get here. That'll give me a few months.'

'I only have six weeks left of my notice.'

She felt the blood drain from her face. 'Six *weeks*?'

'I handed in my notice two weeks ago, and they owed me three weeks' holiday and a whole bunch of time off in lieu, so I told them I'd take the money instead of working my notice.'

She felt her heart pick up as the adrenalin

hit, the reality of her situation suddenly daunting. *Six weeks?* She shrugged again, finding a smile from somewhere. 'That'll still give me a little while to look around. There are always jobs.'

'But not here, not near enough for you to live in your grandfather's house.'

She felt the smile crumble. 'Probably not. Not unless there's a miracle, and I stopped believing in them the day I caught my mother in bed with my boyfriend.'

His eyes widened, and she gave a soft laugh.

'I told you what she was like. She was a stray bullet and she didn't care who got in the way. That time, it was me.'

'Yeah, but—him, too?' He swore softly under his breath. 'That's outrageous, Laura. What the hell were they thinking about? No wonder you were so wary. Only a complete bastard would do that to his girlfriend. And as for your mother...'

'Tell me about it. Anyway, no miracles. We'll be fine.'

'We?'

'Me and Millie.'

'Was she all right when you got home?'

Back to that. 'She was fine. Well, apart from stealing the TV remote. She's a fan of doing that. I found it in the bathroom.'

'Bathroom?'

She shrugged. 'She just hides it. It's a game.'

He smiled fleetingly, then drained his coffee, glanced at his watch and met her eyes again, the smile gone.

'I reckon it's time to go and get the answer,' he said, and she nodded, her heart thudding.

She pushed her cup away and got to her feet. 'Do I look OK? No dog hair or icing sugar?'

His eyes flicked down then back to hers, but he didn't quite veil them in time and she caught a flash of heat.

'No dog hair or icing sugar,' he said, his voice even. 'You look great. What about me? Will I pass?'

She smiled a little sadly, hoping she didn't look bitter.

'Absolutely. You look like a man on his way to the top.'

He held her eyes a fraction longer, then looked away, but not before she saw something in them that she didn't understand.

'Let's go and get this over with, then,' he

said, and she followed him out of the café, wondering what she'd said to put that odd look in his eyes.

All of the odd looks. Funny how she couldn't read him any more.

She was right.

They did offer him the job, and for a moment he felt sick.

'So where does that leave Laura?' he asked, without saying yes or no, but James didn't even blink.

'That's not relevant to this.'

'Yes, it is. Why didn't you offer her the job?'

There was a slight intake of breath from one of the panel and the CEO raised an eyebrow, but James smiled grimly. 'Because, not to put too fine a point on it, you were too good to lose. We need people like you, and we want you in the department.'

'And you don't want Laura?'

'I didn't say that.'

No, and Tom knew he didn't mean it, because they had her anyway. Not that James said so in as many words, but it was a fact.

And he probably *was* better qualified, more experienced, more ready for the role.

He nodded slowly, knowing James was right. Still, for a moment longer he hovered on the brink of turning it down, but he couldn't afford to be that magnanimous. In six weeks he'd be out of work and homeless, so he needed this job at least as much as Laura, however hard-nosed that seemed, but hopefully they'd look after her. It sounded like they would. Well, they'd damn well better. At the very least she needed a stunning reference.

'OK,' he said, swallowing his sense of betrayal. 'I'll take it. Thank you.'

James smiled, his face relaxing. 'You're welcome. It's good to have you. We need to speak to Dr Kemp, and then if you have time we can have a chat about what happens next, so don't go away.'

'I won't.'

The other members of the panel congratulated him, and as he headed for the door James stopped him.

'Don't say anything to Laura. Let me tell her.'

He gave what had to be a slightly bitter smile.

'You probably won't need to. She already told me I'd get it. Just—look after her, please.'

He walked out of the door and she looked up and met his eyes. He could see defeat written on her face, clear as day, and he felt as if he'd betrayed her.

She tilted her chin up, showing her usual courage and stamina. 'You got it, didn't you?'

He didn't answer that. Couldn't. 'They want to talk to you,' he said, his voice a little gruff.

Her smile was a brave attempt. 'Yes, I'm sure they do.'

He swallowed and looked away, and as she passed him she went up on tiptoe and kissed his cheek, her breath soft against his face.

'Congratulations, Dr Stryker. You deserved to win.'

He heard the door close softly behind him, and let out a long, slow breath and rammed his hands in his pockets.

He should have turned it down.

She walked out of the room in a daze, and found Tom still there, standing by the window with his hands in his pockets, staring out across the park, his shoulders rigid.

'Hey.'

'Hey.' He turned slowly towards her, and his eyes looked strangely bleak. 'So what did they say?'

She shrugged. 'I'm not sure. They offered me more locum work, and then James said something about new posts coming up all the time and not to worry, something would turn up in the hospital soon and I would be at the top of their list, but that's just a guess and there's no timescale.'

'Any maternity leave in the pipeline?'

She shook her head. 'Not as far as I know. The only person even remotely likely to go on mat leave hasn't said anything and I'm sure she would have told me before she told James. And there's nobody else of the right grade who's looking to move on as far as I'm aware, at least in the ED. I suppose there's always the various admissions units, but there's nothing advertised and no rumours.'

'So what will you do?'

She shrugged. 'Keep looking. Everyone's desperate for staff so there's bound to be something suitable out there, and for now I'm here.

I'll be covering your job until you start, and there are two people off in April so technically they might want me to cover for them, but beyond that I don't know.' Not that she was particularly happy about still being there after he arrived, but until she found something else...

'So you aren't going to starve?'

She smiled. 'No, Tom, I'm not going to starve, but I might have to kick the house into shape for when I need to move away.' She felt her smile wobble and looked away. 'So, what are you doing now?'

'James wants to talk to me. All the nuts and bolts of when and how, I guess. And then I need to go house-hunting, because I have six weeks to find somewhere to live. I don't suppose you want to help with that?'

She busied herself with her bag. 'Sorry, I can't. I've got to go and walk Millie, then I'm back on duty at one.'

'So I won't see you again.'

'Not till you start, and maybe not then if something else comes up.'

'So I guess this is goodbye, then.'

She heard him move, felt his hands settle on

her shoulders as he turned her into his arms and hugged her firmly against his chest. The scent of his body enveloped her and made her ache for him, but he wasn't hers and never would be, and suddenly she wanted to cry.

'I'm truly sorry, Laura,' he muttered against her hair.

'Don't be, you deserve the job,' she said, and eased out of his arms as James came out of the meeting room. She flashed her boss a smile, reached out and squeezed Tom's arm and met his beautiful eyes for what could be the last time.

'Goodbye, Tom.'

He nodded wordlessly, his eyes filled with something that could have been regret.

Too late for that.

She felt her eyes prickle and turned away, leaving them to their chat and making her way out of the building, across the car park, into her car, down the road. She pulled up on the drive, let herself in, slid down the door and finally, finally gave in to the wrenching sobs that were tearing her apart.

Millie licked her face, and she put her arms around the dog's neck and sobbed into her fur.

'What are we going to do, Millie? Where are we going to live?' she asked brokenly, while Millie whined softly and licked her again.

Then finally she sucked in a breath, straightened up and looked into Millie's anxious eyes. 'We'll be OK,' she promised, and she wasn't sure which of them she was trying to convince.

'Can we have a word?'

James was standing in the door of his office waiting for her, and she went in with him and pasted on a smile, but it was a pretty sketchy effort.

He closed the door and searched her eyes. 'Are you all right, Laura?'

'I'll live.'

'I don't doubt it, but this is not at all the way I wanted it. I'm so, so sorry.'

She shrugged. 'Don't be, James. You had to take him, I know that. He was the best candidate.'

'Actually, he wasn't. He has more experience, but other than that there was nothing between you—but we had you already, and if we gave you the job we'd lose Tom. This way, unless you find something else, we can find a way to keep you here until such time as a suitable vacancy occurs.'

'And if it doesn't?'

'It will.' He hesitated, as if he wanted to tell her something, then dropped his eyes. 'Something will turn up, it always does. We'll still need you for another month after Tom starts on the first of April, and who knows what'll happen in the meantime. At some point soon, there *will* be a job with your name on it.'

And she'd still be here when Tom started work. She didn't know whether to laugh or cry. 'You can't know that.'

He opened his mouth to speak, but the Tannoy burst into life.

'Adult trauma call, five minutes. Adult trauma call, ten minutes.'

'Well, that's our afternoon sorted,' James said with a wry smile, and headed for Resus to prepare for the incoming patients.

So that was that. No time for wallowing in self-pity, no more tears or wasted emotion. Just business as usual.

She sucked in a breath and followed him.

* * *

'Fancy a coffee and a catch up?'

Laura smiled, hoping her concern didn't show in her eyes. She hadn't seen Livvy since the interviews because their shifts hadn't coincided, but she'd been looking pale and strained for weeks now, and she was worried about her. *Please, let it not be her cancer back...*

She pinned on a cheery smile, scribbled her signature and slapped the file shut. 'Yeah, sure. I was just going on my break. Park Café?'

'That would be lovely.'

She ordered a cappuccino and Livvy picked up a luminous green smoothie, and they headed for the same table she'd sat at with Tom just a week ago. She was doing her best to put him out of her mind, but she was failing miserably, and the table didn't help.

Livvy prodded her smoothie with the straw. 'I'm really sorry you didn't get the job. When does this Tom guy start?'

'April Fool's Day.'

'So soon?'

'Yup.' Just five more weeks, and she had no idea how she was going to deal with it.

'Wow, and you're covering Andy and Sam,

so you'll still be here. Are you OK with that, working with the person who got your job? Because I wouldn't be.'

She let out a tiny laugh. 'Honestly? I have no idea.'

'It must be hard not to hate him.'

Hate him? No, she could never hate him. She just wished the ache would go away. She shook her head.

'I don't hate him.'

'Then you're a better person than me. I was gutted for you. I know how much you wanted that job.'

'I did want it, Livvy, but there's more to it than that. I knew him years ago at uni. We didn't always see eye to eye because we're very different people, but we were friends, and I can't hate him for being better than me. And anyway, in the meantime I'm still here, I still have a job, so I'm grateful for that, but it's only a few weeks, so I need to start looking for another job in earnest.'

'No, don't do that,' Livvy said instantly, and Laura blinked.

'What? Why?'

Livvy shifted, glancing over her shoulder

to check if there was anyone nearby, then she leant forwards, her eyes bright with suppressed emotion, and before Laura could even open her mouth she spoke again, her voice hushed but fizzing with joy.

'I'm pregnant,' she mouthed.

Laura felt her jaw sag, and her eyes welled with tears.

'Oh, Livvy! Oh, that's amazing! I've been so worried. You've been looking peaky and I...' She tailed off, put her coffee down and hugged Livvy hard across the table. 'Oh, I'm so, so happy for you!'

And then a thought popped into her head, bizarre and unlikely, but...

'Does James know?'

Livvy nodded. 'Yes. I had to tell him really early on. That's why I've been working in Minors since New Year, because of the X-rays in Resus, but it's time to go public and I wanted you to know before everyone else. I've been longing to tell you for ages, but I'm thirteen weeks now so I can't really hide it much longer, and I've already told James that if all goes well, I'm going to be leaving, so my job'll be up for grabs. Like, permanently.'

She felt her breath jam in her throat, and her heart lurched. 'Seriously?'

'Seriously. Life's too short, and I want to spend it with the children. Amber and Charlie don't know yet, but they're going to be so excited, and I want to be there with them all. I never thought I'd ever be a mother, and I want to do it properly and be the best mum I can to all of them, and Matt's right behind me, so it's the right thing for all of us. And I've told James he's got to give you my job, so I hope you and Tom can bury your differences and work together.'

She laughed, but in the background her thoughts were tumbling. It would mean she wouldn't have to move out of the house, wouldn't have to find another job elsewhere, another house, another dog walker for Millie—if it came off. If everything was all right with Livvy's baby, and if she got the job.

A lot of ifs, all resulting in one inevitable fact.

She'd be working alongside Tom.

Tom, who twelve years ago had winkled a way into her heart, and just a week ago had stolen it, along with her job. Or not her job, as it turned out...

Could she honestly work with him on a permanent basis? And if she did, what about their very personal relationship? Was that always going to be in the way?

Maybe she *should* be looking elsewhere, instead of waiting for Livvy's job which she might not even get.

How could it all get so complicated?

Five weeks later...

So, it was done.

In a whirlwind six weeks he'd bought a house, all his personal possessions were relocated, unpacked and put away, and he'd even been organised enough to get an internet food order delivered last night.

And today—in half an hour, to be exact—he started work as Senior Specialist Registrar in the ED in Yoxburgh Park Hospital.

New house, new job—new life?

He could only hope so. The last one hadn't proved to be so great, and the success of this one—well, that might depend on all sorts of things other than Laura, but she seemed to be all he could think about. Was she still there? Would he see her again?

He had no idea, but his heart was doing a little jig behind his ribs and it was getting on his nerves. He didn't want to be thinking about Laura. He didn't want to be thinking about anything today except finding his feet in a new team, a new department, a new hospital.

And Laura—well, there was nothing he could do about Laura. He'd spent the past six weeks thinking about her, worrying about how she was, if she'd found another job, if he'd see her again. Today would bring some of those answers, and he just hoped they'd be answers he could live with.

With any luck she wouldn't still be here, because if he knew one thing after that night it was that once wasn't enough, but she'd made it clear it wasn't going anywhere and he was done with unrequited lust.

Still, maybe she wouldn't be there, and as for what his future held, he had bigger things to worry about. He'd made an appointment with an optometrist for tomorrow which might give him some answers, and until then he wasn't going to think about his eyes. Or about Laura. Just his new job.

He straightened the mirror on the wall, stood back and studied himself briefly and gave a tiny nod. He'd do.

Hefting his keys in his hand, he let himself out of his new front door—which was sticking; he'd have to do something about that, and the leaky shower hose and a few hundred other things—and set off for the hospital.

It was a mile, by his calculations, so would take him fifteen or twenty minutes. That was fine. Perfect, in fact. Enough to get his body moving, not so far he'd be tempted to take the car unless the weather was horrendous, which it wasn't.

It was an unseasonably gorgeous day, the sun shining down on him, birds twittering in the trees and hedges of the gardens he passed, the traffic very light on the quiet residential streets that led to the hospital.

So much better than fighting for a space on the Underground, jostling on the pavements, dodging through crowds on his daily commute in London. And if he breathed in deeply, he could smell the sea.

It was going to be good living here, he could feel it already. So long as Laura was all right. *Please let her be all right...*

'Laura, I hate to do this but can I ask you a massive favour?'

'Depends what it is,' she said, her heart sinking because the date was etched on her psyche and she hadn't slept a wink, so she knew what was coming.

So did James, because his smile was wry and a little harassed. 'Tom starts today, and Sam's tied up in Resus, I've got a meeting I can't get out of, and with Andy off I just can't spare the time. If you could take him under your wing, that would be a huge help.'

Great. It wasn't enough that he'd stolen her job. Now she had to babysit him, show him how to do the job she'd been doing, the job she'd wanted, and all the time the memories of that night were going to be right there in her face.

Great. Just great. And on April Fool's Day, of all days. Someone was having a laugh at her expense.

'Sure,' she said calmly. 'No worries.' Just a

whole bunch more angst. 'What time does he start?'

'Eight. He's done HR and all that stuff yesterday, so it's just a case of settling in. I don't want to throw him in at the deep end on his first day.'

She would have been quite happy to do that. She was torn between aching to see him again and running a mile, neither of which would get the job done.

'Don't worry, James, I'll look after him. I'm sure he'll be fine. And talk of the devil,' she added, glancing past James and meeting those beautiful eyes across the central work station.

Tom smiled at her, but it didn't quite reach his eyes, and she didn't imagine hers did, either. She had no idea how he was going to react to her still being there, and she had a horrible feeling it was going to be even more awkward than before. Especially if her heart kept leaping about like this every time she caught sight of him.

James turned, his smile far more spontaneous and welcoming. 'Tom! Good to see you! Look, I'm really sorry, I'm going to have to abandon you, but Laura's promised to look after you and I'll be back as soon as I can. It's all a bit crazy today.'

'When isn't it?' Tom said drily, his smile relaxing a little, and after a few seconds of chat James headed off and left them alone together and Tom turned back to meet her eyes.

'Hello, Laura.'

Her heart slammed against her ribs and then lodged in her throat, and she swallowed hard. 'Hi. Are you all set?'

He nodded, his eyes searching her face. 'You're still here. I wasn't sure if you would be.'

She tried to smile. 'Nor was I, but it seems I am, at least for now. Shall we go? There's a patient in Resus with Sam, and unless I'm mistaken that's the red phone ringing, so we'll have another incoming in a minute.'

His eyes searched hers thoughtfully, but he just nodded and followed her without a word. They passed Livvy, who met her eyes, obviously worried, and she threw her a reassuring smile and pushed open the door to Resus. The team already in there glanced up and greeted him with smiles of welcome, and she turned to look at Tom.

'OK, so this is Resus. We have four beds in here, all fully equipped for anything we might need, and we also have Paeds Resus next door but we don't tend to get involved with that. I'm sure the kit is all pretty standard.'

'Yes, it looks it. Better give me a quick tour so I can hit the ground running.'

She did that, all the while so conscious of his body close to hers, waiting for the Tannoy to free her. She showed him where all the scrubs and other PPE were, and then the speaker burst into life as she'd expected.

'Adult trauma call, five minutes. Paediatric Trauma call, five minutes.'

'Parent and child?' he asked softly, and she shrugged.

'Better go and find out. Here, take these scrubs. It could get messy. The locker room's at the end of the corridor on the left. Come back as soon as you're done. I'll brief the team.'

He was right, it was a mother and child with leg injuries, both knocked down by a car on the school run, and the mother was beside herself despite a very serious open fracture of her lower leg.

'I want to see my son—he'll need me!' she sobbed, clutching at Laura, and she took her hand and held it tight.

'Rory's in good hands, Sarah,' she said calmly, 'and your husband's on his way in, but we need to get your leg sorted out and check the rest of you over. My name's Laura, and this is Tom. We're both doctors. Tom, do you want to lead?'

'Sure. If I do the primary survey can you take a look at that foot, please and get some X-rays? Better draw up some ketamine ready. And can we fast bleep the orthopaedic reg?'

'Done it. They're on their way.'

'Thanks. Hi, Sarah, my name's Tom. Mind if I have a look at you?'

He started the primary survey while Laura moved to examine Sarah's leg, and after a moment she began to relax. He was good. Very good. Kind, gentle, patient, thorough—the sort of doctor she'd want looking after her under those circumstances. And he was good with the team, too.

She glanced up and met Sam's eyes, and he smiled and nodded in silent agreement. Good.

He was confident in Tom's ability, and so he should be.

Gone was the cocky young man who'd treated life as a playground. In his place was a calm, measured professional, capable and sympathetic without shirking the tough stuff. He needed to be, because Sarah's ankle was a mess and the X-ray did nothing to reassure Laura.

'Cap refill?' he asked, still working his way down her body, and she shook her head.

'No pedal pulse. We can't really wait for Ortho,' she murmured softly, and he glanced at the X-ray, nodded and bent over their patient so she could see his face.

'OK, Sarah, we've got a bit of a problem here. You've got quite a nasty fracture just above your ankle, and your foot's not in the right position so we need to do something to straighten it. We're going to give you something to make you drowsy first, then once we've sorted it we can get you to Theatre so they can fix it properly. Can someone called the orthopaedic registrar again, please? This is going to need surgery promptly. And can someone get the plaster ready, please?' He picked up the ketamine syringe. 'Right, Sarah, this is going to make you really sleepy so you won't feel a thing. Can I have someone on the airway?'

He gave her the ketamine, and the moment she was under Tom took hold of her foot. 'Ready?'

Laura nodded and held her knee, and he pulled, steadily and firmly, and the bones slid back into place.

'Pulse check?' he said without letting go, and she threaded her fingers between his on Sarah's foot and nodded.

'Pedal pulse. It's not massive, but it's there, and cap refill's three seconds and it's pinking up. Well done.'

He flashed her a grin and looked at the nurse waiting for instructions, the wadding in her hands.

'Right, let's get that on please while I'm holding this in position, and is there any word from Ortho?'

'I'm here,' the orthopaedic registrar said, coming in behind him, and she took a look at what he'd done and smiled. 'Good job. Want to work in Orthopaedics?'

He grinned at her and shook his head. 'Not particularly. Would you like to get some gloves on and take this over from me while it sets?'

'Sure. We need X-rays, and let's get her some fluids on board and then we can take her straight up to Theatre.'

He stepped back and left her to it, then turned to Laura.

'Can you see if there's any news on the son? It would be nice to be able to reassure her.'

'Sure. I'll go and have a look.'

She left him and went through to Paeds Resus, and found Ed Shackleton, one of the consultant paediatricians, working on a small boy of about five who was crying for his mother.

'Is that Rory?'

'Yes—how's mum?'

'Off to Theatre soon for surgery to her leg but otherwise OK. How's he?'

'Sore and scraped, but remarkably un- scathed. He's been lucky, I would say.'

'What, lucky for somebody who's been hit by a car?' she said with wry grin, and he chuckled.

'Yeah, that kind of lucky. Hey, Rory, Laura's been looking after your mummy. Do you want to talk to her?'

He nodded and sniffled, and she took his hand gently. 'Mummy's going to be OK, Rory. She's hurt her leg, too, but she's going to be OK. The doctors are looking after her now.'

'I want Mummy,' he sobbed, and she smoothed the hair back from his forehead.

'I know you do, sweetheart, and we'll fix that as soon as we can. He's got a bruise on his head,' she added over her shoulder, and Ed nodded.

'He's got bruises all over. We're going to admit him for observation. Dad's on the way in to see him.'

'Don't let him hang about, then, the ortho's already here and they're taking her to Theatre very soon.'

She went back and found Sarah was still there with her husband now, so she had a chance to reassure them both.

Sarah's eyes filled at the news. 'Thank you...'

'Yes, thank you,' her husband echoed, his shoulders sagging in relief, and he kissed Sarah goodbye as she was wheeled off to Theatre, and then he turned to Laura. 'I need to see my son,' he said, shaking visibly, and she smiled.

'Of course you do. If you come with me I'll take you to him.'

'Thank you—and thank you all so much for looking after Sarah.'

She smiled. 'It's what we're here for,' she said softly, and took him through to Paeds.

CHAPTER FOUR

IT FELT LIKE the longest day of her life.

James didn't reappear until nearly twelve, so she had four hours of babysitting Tom—which was fine while they were busy, but then suddenly there'd be a lull, and there it was again, the elephant in the room.

Another elephant this time, not the 'why did you change your mind' one, but the 'we finally gave in and had the most amazing sex *ever*' one, trumpeting its head off every time she caught his eye. So much for closure.

Had she known—had she had the slightest *inkling*—that they'd end up working together, she would have run a mile that night. More. But she hadn't. She'd assumed it would be the end of it, that one or other of them would be there, but not both. Never both.

Working alongside him was going to be so hard when all she wanted was to be with him, the last person in the world she needed in her life, another self-confessed free spirit like her mother… And then, just to turn the screw, there was Livvy's job waiting for her in the wings, a permanent SpR job just a grade under Tom's, the sort of job she'd had before she'd had to drop everything and come to look after Grumps. The only downside was that she'd have to work alongside Tom, and she wasn't sure she'd ever be OK with that.

Oh, Grumps, where are you when I need you to talk some sense into me?

'Sorry? Were you talking to me?'

Had she really said that? 'No, I was thinking out loud. Look, why don't you go and grab a coffee?'

Or just go, really. Anywhere would do until she could sort her head out.

'I don't need a coffee.'

'Are you sure?'

'Positive.' He tipped his head on one side and eyed her thoughtfully. 'Is this going to be difficult?' he murmured.

And there it was again, loud and proud, and this time the elephant had a voice. She didn't bother to ask what he meant.

She met his eyes again and found—sympathy?

'No,' she said, and realised it was true. The working thing anyway. She already knew that was fine. 'It's just…'

'Awkward.'

That word again. Like at the interview, but with bells on.

'Yes, frankly. It is. I don't have a choice, I have to work, but I wasn't expecting we'd be working together and if I'd known, there's no way I would have—'

She cut herself off, but he understood all too perfectly, judging by the look in his eyes.

'No, but we did, so we have to deal with it and move on. As you said, closure, and I'm fine with that, I have no regrets, but just so you know, given the same circumstances I'd do it again in a heartbeat.'

His eyes spoke volumes, and she sucked in her breath and looked away, her body leaping to life, every sense heightened. She could feel his warmth, smell the intoxicating scent of his skin, see the slow, steady rise and fall of his chest. And she had to get away from him.

'They aren't the same, though. The circumstances.'

'No, they're not, so we have to find a way to put it behind us so we can work together without this constant tension.'

She looked around, her heart pounding, hoping there was nobody in earshot.

'Seriously, Tom, we can't talk about this here,' she muttered. 'Go and get a coffee while it's quiet.'

He sucked in his breath, his eyes laughing. 'Oh, Laura. Tempting fate? You must be desperate to get rid of me.'

'Don't be ridiculous—'

'Adult trauma call, ten minutes. Adult trauma call, fifteen minutes.'

She closed her eyes and he half groaned, half laughed.

'There you go. Works like magic every time. I'm sure you did that on purpose.'

He was properly laughing at her now, his eyes doing that sexy crinkling thing, and suddenly the prospect of being stuck right beside him again for hours wanting him like this was all too much. 'I don't have time for this,' she said shortly, and squeezed past him and headed in the other direction.

'Hey, that's not Resus! Where are you going?'

She didn't even look back. 'The loo. We could be in there for hours.'

And even if they weren't, she needed to give herself a severe talking-to in the mirror.

He watched her walk away, her body hidden by the scrubs, but not successfully because he knew now what they were hiding. Knew every curve and contour, every dip, every hollow.

The feel of her abdomen, soft yet taut, the swell of her breasts a perfect fit for his hands, the way the pulse at the base of her throat beat under his tongue. The arch of her back as she bucked against his hand, the whisper of her breath against his skin...

'Right, I'm back. Sorry about that. How've you got on?'

Damn. He hauled in a breath and turned to his new boss, hoping his expression wasn't a total mess.

'Fine. All good.'

'And Laura?'

Ah. Laura. How *was* Laura? 'She's OK.'

James scanned his face. 'Good. I was a bit concerned. She was pretty gutted that you got the job, so I was very conscious of that when

I left you together but unfortunately I didn't have a choice. Anyway, whatever. Did I hear a trauma call?'

'Yes, two. I was just heading to Resus. Laura's following me.'

'We'll take the first one, then. Laura can join us with Sam in a minute.'

Good. He wouldn't be crushed up against her again, so he could have some breathing space and try and get his mind and body under control before he disgraced himself.

So much for closure...

She was heading home some time after six when he fell in beside her.

'Can we talk?'

Him again, just when she thought she'd have some peace. 'Not really. I need to get home to take Millie for a walk.'

'Mind if I walk with you, then?'

'Well, I can't really stop you.'

'You could, but I'd rather you didn't, because I do think we need to discuss how we're going to manage this, or working together's going to be really difficult.'

Going to be? She stopped in her tracks and

turned to face him. 'What is there to discuss, Tom? We slept together, and now we're working together and yes, it's awkward, but we're stuck with it. There's nothing more to say.'

'Are you sure about that?'

'Well, yes. What else is there? It's over. We've dealt with it. We need to move on.'

He studied her for a moment before he answered, his voice soft and oddly sad. 'Yes, we do, and I know we can't turn the clock back but we do need to find some middle ground, rediscover our friendship if nothing else.'

Friendship? Friendship was the last thing on her mind. All she wanted to do was tear his clothes off, and that was so not going to happen! She should never have slept with him. Idiot.

'Do we have to do this tonight? Millie's waiting for her walk and I need to get home,' she muttered, setting off again, but he was still beside her, making all her nerve endings tingle.

'I'm going this way anyway,' he said. 'My house is in Brooke Avenue.'

Seriously? That was right round the corner from her! Great. Marvellous.

'Actually, I could do with some local knowledge. The front door sticks and I'm worried I'm going to break the glass if I keep forcing it. Any idea where I can get some tools so I can free it off a bit? A plane, maybe? Sandpaper, even.'

'You don't have any tools?'

'Why would I need them? I had a brand new flat. I didn't even need to pick up a paintbrush.'

She stopped again, giving up any hope of distancing herself from him. 'So what do you need?'

He shrugged. 'A plane, a rasp, sandpaper? Maybe a screwdriver to take the door off its hinges?'

'I've got all of those. Give me time to walk Millie. I'll come round with them—seven o'clock, seven thirty?'

'Are you sure?'

No, she wasn't, but she'd said it now. 'Yes, I'm sure. You could get us a takeaway if you like. I haven't got anything in the fridge so I was going to have to go shopping. What number are you? Give me your address, I'll come round straight after our walk.'

'It's number forty-two, Brooke Avenue.

Bring her with you if you like. You don't want to leave her alone again.'

'Oh—OK. Thanks. I'll do that.'

Why did he have to do that? Be considerate and think about the dog? Just when she was trying to convince herself she didn't like him...

She deliberately took a different route at the next junction, partly to give herself some breathing space and partly because she didn't want him knowing exactly where she lived, because she wouldn't trust him not to rock up at any time and unravel her all over again. Not that it could get much more complicated.

'I'll see you later,' she said, and walked away, hoping to goodness he didn't decide to follow her.

Tom watched her go, her back ramrod straight, and let out his breath on a long, thoughtful huff.

Awkward didn't even begin to touch it. She was so prickly, so tense, so—so *un-Laura*—that he almost wished he hadn't slept with her.

Almost. But he couldn't wish that away, in all honesty, even though it hadn't heralded a new beginning for them but an ending, at last, to whatever it was they'd had. A tying up of loose ends, she'd called it at the time, and that left a sick, hollow feeling in his gut because he'd realised afterwards that he didn't want to tie up their loose ends. He wanted to unravel them more, not have closure.

Except she did, and he had to respect that, but maybe they could be friends again, if he could only keep his mind off that night and his body under control.

He really shouldn't have taken the job.

He let himself in, giving the door an extra shove with his foot, and then it wouldn't close so he swore and kicked it shut in frustration, making the glass rattle.

Stupid thing. It only needed a bit off the side down at the bottom, but he'd fallen at the first hurdle. Not that he missed the flat. He'd never been happy there, and he'd left it and all its contents behind without a pang of regret. Including Karen, but that was fine. He had bigger fish to fry right now than a cheating lover and a disloyal boss with the morals of an alley cat.

And now he was here, in Yoxburgh, making a new start in a charming little cottage the antithesis of his sharply modern London flat, a bit run down but perfect for him, and he could do it up as he went along—well, once he'd bought some tools. It'd keep him off the streets, at least, and might give him something other than Laura to fret about.

And on the subject of Laura...

He was starving, and he imagined she was, too, as they hadn't had time to stop all day, and his fridge was full. If he did nothing else, he could make her something nice to eat rather than getting a takeaway. That might break the ice.

He went to inspect the contents of his kitchen, turned on the oven, relieved that it worked, made a pasta bake packed with veg in a cheesy tomato sauce, put it in the oven and ran upstairs, had a quick rinse in the leaky shower, pulled on some clean clothes and went down in time to check the pasta bake.

Perfect. He opened the front door a bit so she could come in, threw a salad together and tidied up while he waited.

She hadn't known what to expect, but it wasn't the run-down little Edwardian cottage between numbers forty and forty-four which had been on the market for ages. She found the old brass numbers buried in ivy on the gatepost, so it must be right.

She rang the bell even though the door was ajar, and it swung open to reveal Tom looking super-sexy in jeans and a blinding white shirt, his feet enticingly bare.

Why was she here? She must be crazy.

Too late to run away.

He stepped back with a smile that threatened to unravel her and beckoned her in. 'Hi. Welcome to my new home. Hello, Millie. Do you remember me?'

The dog went straight up to him, smiling and wagging and wiggling with delight, and Laura followed her over the threshold to the smell of something delicious that made her stomach growl and her mouth water.

It wasn't the only amazing aroma hanging in the air, because Tom was smelling every bit as enticing. She kicked off her shoes and put them beside the door in case they were dirty, although the carpet had seen better days anyway.

'Did you find me all right?' he asked, looking up from fussing Millie, and she nodded.

'Yes, once I found the number under the ivy.'

'Yeah, I keep meaning to cut it away but I haven't had the time or the tools.'

'Talking of which,' she said, and handed him a groaning carrier bag. 'I wasn't sure what you'd need, but I put a paintbrush and some primer undercoat in there as well as the tools.'

'Brilliant. Thank you so much. I'll let you have them back as soon as I've done it.'

'No rush,' she said, glancing around and smiling. 'You might need them again any minute.'

He laughed and rolled his eyes. 'I might well. Come on in, I'll get you a drink.'

He shoved the door shut with his foot and led her through to the sitting room, and Laura slowed to a halt and looked around her in amazement.

'Wow. It's like a time warp.'

'Yes, it is. The executors were going to get a house clearance firm to take it all away but I didn't have any furniture or kitchen stuff—nothing, really, and they were desperate to sell so they were happy to throw it all in with the price, which saved me having to worry about that immediately, at least.'

Sell? 'You've bought the house? That was quick. I assumed they'd decided to rent it.'

'No, I bought it,' he said, putting paid to any hope she might have had that he wasn't putting down roots. 'I had the cash in the bank and it went through really quickly, and I got the keys two days ago. Come on through. I hope you're hungry, I had tons of food so I've made us a pasta bake.'

Her stomach growled again, and she gave up any idea of resistance.

'It smells amazing. I'm ravenous.'

'Good. So am I. Let's eat it before it gets cold.'

She was all for that. It gave them something to do before the conversation that she could feel looming in the wings, but there was only so long you could drag out a bowl of pasta and a handful of salad leaves. She even had seconds—anything rather than run out of excuses to stall what was coming.

But finally there was nothing left to eat, nothing left to do, and he picked up their plates, put them in the sink and came back with the wine bottle to top up their glasses.

'Let's go in the sitting room.'

It wasn't a question, so she got up and followed him, Millie at her heels. He sat at one end of the sofa, and she sat at the other end, her feet curled up under her, nursing the glass of wine, cradling it in her hands and staring down into it as if it held the answer to the universe while he sat in silence, fondling Millie's ears as she leant against his leg.

Was he ever going to start talking? Or was he waiting for her—in which case he'd wait for ever because this was his idea and she wanted to know what he was going to say.

Except he didn't. He asked, instead.

'Talk to me, Laura,' he said gently. 'I need to know where you stand on our relationship because we have to sort this out.'

She looked up then, slightly startled.

'What relationship?'

He gave a slightly disbelieving little laugh. '*What* relationship? Um, let me see now… How about our friendship? Or the fact that we're working together now? That's a relationship, and apparently an awkward one. And then there's the fact that we slept together,' he added after a slight pause, and she felt herself colour slightly and looked away.

'That shouldn't have happened.'

'Maybe not, but it did, and as I said before, I don't regret it, but I don't think it's dealt with. I don't think it tied up any loose ends at all. I think it unravelled them all a bit more and now it's just a mess that we have to sort out.'

She looked back at him, confused now. 'How are they unravelled?'

'Because I can't get you out of my mind?' he said softly. 'I never could, and that was before I knew what I was missing.'

She felt her heart thump. 'So what are you suggesting?'

'I don't know. Do you think we can find a way forward and be friends again? And if not, what?'

She shrugged. 'I don't know. It wouldn't go anywhere, anyway. You don't do relationships. You never have done. Look at all those girls in college.'

'They were the wrong people.'

'So why sleep with them in the first place if they were wrong?' she asked bluntly.

He held her eyes, then looked away himself this time. 'Maybe because the right person wouldn't have me?'

Did he mean her?

She waited, but he didn't say anything more, and the silence stretched between them for an age before she cracked.

He couldn't mean her... 'I wasn't the right person,' she said tightly, her voice low and unsteady, her heart pounding.

He looked back at her, his eyes searching. She told herself to relax, but she couldn't. Not when he was studying her, reading her awkward body language, the tense, tight posture, the fast, shallow breathing that she couldn't control.

'Weren't you?' he murmured, his voice gentle, and her heart tumbled in her chest.

'No!'

'Are you sure? Because I'm not.'

She made herself meet his eyes again, shoring up her defences because she knew what she'd see in them. 'No. You were a heartbreaker, Tom, and I didn't need my heart broken. I still don't.'

He sighed and dropped his head back. 'Laura,

I didn't want to break your heart. I don't. That's not me.'

'Oh, tell it to the fairies, Tom! I was there, I saw you in action, and I saw the girls who loved you. They all wanted you to love them back, and you never did. You didn't even have a clue.'

He studied her thoughtfully. 'Did you love me, Laura?' he asked her softly, totally taking her by surprise, and she coloured and looked away, her heart pounding.

'Of course I didn't love you! I had too much self-respect, and I didn't want my heart broken. Still don't.'

He shook his head. 'I didn't set out to break any hearts, and I never made anybody any promises. I made sure they knew I wasn't looking for a relationship. I wanted to be a doctor, and not just a doctor, the best doctor I could be. So I didn't want any distractions, I didn't want any angst, I just wanted a bit of fun from time to time, like all the other lads, and the rest of the time I worked. You know that. You saw me. You were always in the library.'

She had been, and she'd worked as hard as him. Harder, probably.

'Did you do it just to annoy me?'

'What, go out with the girls?'

'No. Work in the library.'

He smiled a little wryly. 'No. I did it because I knew you would be there.'

She held his eyes, spellbound for a moment, then looked away and took a gulp of her wine. 'That's rubbish. Why would you do that?'

'Because it gave me a legitimate reason to be near you? I wanted you, Laura. You fascinated me. You gave so little away, but there was so much there, and you wouldn't let me in. Why? Was it because of what your mother did, the way she behaved?'

Was it? Was he right? Did she judge him so harshly because she saw him in the same light as her? The mother she'd caught in bed with her boyfriend? The mother who'd dragged her all over the place as a child, camping at festivals where she'd have to listen to her and some random stranger making—no, not making love, there was never any love. Just sex, for the sake of it, when they'd thought she was asleep.

'I don't know. Maybe. I know I was never close to her. She never seemed to want me, and she didn't make any concessions, she just did what she wanted. I don't think she's ever loved me. I don't think she knows how to love,' she said quietly, holding back sudden tears that didn't seem to want to be held back.

'Oh, Laura...'

She squeezed her eyes shut, felt the sofa dip beside her as his arm went round her shoulders. Felt the wine glass carefully eased out of her fingers, heard the clink as he put it down on the glass-topped table, felt the warmth of his breath against her cheek as he held her close.

'Tell me about her,' he said softly, so she told him. She told him about the festivals, about the beach-front cabins in Goa and Thailand, little more than open shelters, about the times she'd pressed her hands to her ears so she didn't have to hear what her mother was doing with men she didn't even know.

The drugs, the disruptive lifestyle, the uncertainty, the open relationships in a commune where she'd never felt truly safe...

'My grandparents took me in when I was ten,' she said, scrubbing at her face and sniffing. 'I was supposed to be going to Glastonbury with my mother but I didn't want to go and I told them why, and they were furious with her and there was a lot of shouting. She told them they were welcome to me, and she went without me, so they kept me, even though Grandma was very ill by then. They gave me a proper home for the first time in my life, sent me to school, fed me, cared for me, loved me, and when she died Grumps put me into boarding school. He thought it would be better for me but I hated it, so he got me into our local high school and I lived with him until I was eighteen.

'He was the father I never had, the mother I needed, the only friend who ever really understood me. He filled all the gaps in my education, and more, while my mother just flittered in and out of my life like a malevolent fairy. He was so kind, so wise, so understanding. And I miss him—I miss him so much...'

The tears were streaming down her cheeks now, and he cradled her wordlessly against his chest and rocked her, while Millie pressed her cold wet nose against her hand and licked it.

Then she hauled herself together, sat up and

swiped the tears off her cheeks and gave Millie a little stroke.

'Sorry. I didn't mean to do that.'

'It's fine. You needed it. I always knew he was very important to you, I just didn't realise why.'

She nodded, sniffing, and rummaged in her pocket for a tissue to blow her nose. 'I'm sorry. It's just self-indulgence.'

'That's not illegal, you know,' he said, his voice gently teasing, and she laughed.

'No, I know, but...' She shrugged. 'You're right, my reaction to you probably was because of my mother, I just didn't realise. You were no different to the other guys at college, and lots of them were worse than you. None of you were a patch on my mother, but maybe I've always judged you so harshly because of the way she behaved. It just hit a nerve, I guess, but I didn't realise it had affected me so much.'

'It wouldn't be surprising if it had,' he said, a thread of anger in his voice. 'I can't believe she did all that to you. She had no right to do that, no right to expose you to things like that.'

'Oh, Mel thought everything had an educational value.'

'Mel?'

'My mother. I never called her Mummy or Mum or anything like that. She wouldn't let me. She said it was ageing. She was only seventeen when I was born, and I was just an inconvenience, to be honest.'

'What about your father?'

'What about him? I don't suppose she has any more idea who he is than I do.'

She heard him swear very softly under his breath. 'Do you ever see her now?'

She shook her head. 'No. She missed Grumps' funeral. She didn't know he'd died—didn't look at her email which is the only way I can ever get hold of her. She saw it eventually and rocked up four weeks later with a load of luggage, and said she'd come home.'

'Home?'

He sounded shocked, and she laughed. 'Yes. That's what I thought. I told her it wasn't her home, hadn't been for years, and he'd left it to me. And I told her I never wanted to see her again, and shut the door.'

'But she's your mother, Laura.'

'No, she's not. She hasn't earned the right to be called a mother. She's the woman who gave birth to the child of a random stranger. Nothing more.'

She sucked in a deep breath and straightened up. 'I need to go home. It's getting late and I've got to be at work at six tomorrow.'

'Yeah, me, too. I'll walk you home.'

'You don't need to do that!'

'Yes, I do. You're not walking home in the dark, and anyway, it's the easiest way to show me where you live, so I can return those tools when I'm done.'

She hesitated, then gave him a rueful little smile. 'OK. Thank you.'

'My pleasure. Come on, let's go.'

He used his phone as a torch and they walked along the quiet dimly lit streets, turning left, then right, then left again, and she stopped outside a bungalow with a pretty front garden.

'This is me,' she said.

'I'll see you in,' he said firmly, and she laughed.

'Just like Grumps.'

'I'll take that as a compliment,' he murmured, and she smiled up at him.

'Yeah. I guess in a way it is.'

She slid her key in the lock and opened the door, then turned off the burglar alarm as it started beeping.

'Thank you for feeding me, I was really hungry.'

'It was the least I could do to thank you for babysitting me all day.'

She smiled. 'Well, it was a good choice, then. I'd forgotten how good your pasta bakes are.'

He threw her a wry grin. 'Another compliment. Wonders will never cease.' He frowned slightly and hesitated before he spoke again. 'We are going to be all right at work, aren't we?' he asked, and she pulled a rueful face and smiled at him.

'I think so. I'm glad we cleared the air.'

'Yeah, me too.'

He took a step closer and cradled her cheek in his hand, and she tilted her face up to meet his eyes.

'Goodnight, Laura. I'll see you tomorrow.'

He touched his lips to hers in a fleeting kiss and then stepped back before he could give in to the urge to kiss her properly, because he knew it wouldn't end there. Tonight wasn't the time for that, and maybe it never would be.

She smiled a little sadly, as if she was echoing his thoughts. 'Goodnight, Tom. And thanks again.'

She called Millie inside, stepped back and closed the door, and he walked home, still burning with anger after her revelations about her mother. He'd known she wasn't great, but—wow. She'd been spectacularly bad.

No kid should have to put up with that. No wonder Laura had been so hard on him. He just hoped she would give him a chance to prove that he wasn't like that, that he was different to her mother, very different, because suddenly, for some reason, her opinion of him mattered more than it ever had and closure was the last thing on his mind.

He reached his drive, and as he put his phone away and reached for his keys, he tripped over the front doorstep and slammed against the door. It was the second time he'd stumbled on the way home, and he felt a flicker of dread.

He found the keyhole, turned the key in the door, pushed it open with a shove and used his foot to squeeze it shut. He'd have to sort it out tomorrow, otherwise he'd trash the door completely and probably break the old stained glass. And then he could return her tools, and maybe she'd return the favour and invite him in for a meal, and then…

No. Bad idea—especially until he knew what was going on with his eyes. Tomorrow. He'd find out tomorrow, and until then he wasn't going to think about it. It was probably nothing. He went through to the kitchen, loaded the elderly dishwasher, switched it on and went to bed, only to wake with a pounding heart in a tangle of bedding, the remnants of the nightmare still vivid in his mind.

What's wrong with my eyes?

CHAPTER FIVE

IT GALLED HER, but he'd been absolutely right.

They'd needed that conversation, and it had made a huge difference to them working together. Gone was the tension—or at least, *that* tension—and the elephant was back in the jungle where it belonged.

Yes, she still found him ridiculously sexy and appealing, yes, she still wanted him, but more than that she wanted his friendship. He knew more about her now than anyone else ever had apart from Grumps, and she knew more about him than she had, which had made her look at him in a new and rather kinder light.

He'd been a good friend, a better friend perhaps than she'd deserved, and she'd forgotten that. And shortly into their shift, she was reminded of something else she'd forgotten: he had a wicked sense of fun and wasn't beyond using it on her.

Her patient was a man in his late seventies

with vague symptoms that he seemed unwilling to clarify but which could have indicated a prostate problem, so she needed to examine him and he refused to let her.

'I don't need to be inspected by a nurse,' he growled. 'I want a doctor.'

She hung onto her temper and smiled reassuringly. 'I am a doctor, Mr Jones. I've told you that.'

He glanced at her lanyard, unimpressed. 'Well, I want a proper doctor, someone with a bit of experience. Someone like him,' he said, and pointed.

She turned, and Tom appeared at her side, his mouth twitching just the teeniest bit.

'Did you want me, sir?'

'Yes, you can take over from this young woman.'

'Oh, I'm sorry, I'm rather tied up,' he said smoothly. 'What is the problem, exactly?'

'It's not right,' he muttered. 'I'm sure she's a lovely girl, but I've got grandchildren older than her.'

Tom sucked in a slow breath and smiled in a way that made Laura want to laugh out loud. She bit her lip and waited.

'That's nice for you,' Tom murmured. 'However, Dr Kemp is a senior registrar. She's highly qualified and extremely competent, but if it's a case of preferring to be examined by a man rather than a woman, that can be arranged. There's a more junior male doctor but he's tied up right now. He should be free in about half an hour? Or you can let Dr Kemp do it to save you time.'

'Well, what about you? You don't look that tied up,' the man growled, but Tom just smiled that smile again.

'On the contrary, I have a very sick patient whose life I'm in the middle of saving, so I really don't have time. Dr Kemp does, or you could wait for the more junior doctor to see you, but he might well ask her for her opinion anyway. It's up to you.'

And he strode briskly away, leaving Mr Jones to wrestle with his pride, while Laura bit her lip and waited patiently for him to make up his mind.

'So how's the patient whose life you were saving?' she asked when she next caught up with Tom.

His mouth quirked. 'What patient? I was coming to see if you had time for a coffee.'

'What? You just abandoned me with him!'

His grin didn't have a scrap of contrition about it. 'Yes, because I wasn't going to give him the satisfaction and I knew you were perfectly capable of dealing with him.'

'Well, cheers for that. You could have spared us both the humiliation.'

'So what happened in the end? Did he let you look at him?'

'Oh, yes, after he'd swallowed his pride. He was just hideously embarrassed. Apparently he's taken up internet dating and was having unprotected sex. It looked like classic gonorrhoea, so I took some swabs for confirmation, gave him an antibiotic injection, a prescription for a follow-up tablet and a stern lecture about safe sex, and referred him to Sexual Health for contact tracing. Oh, and eye drops. He'd managed to give himself conjunctivitis from it.'

'I'm glad you picked up on that. I did wonder if you would.'

She stared at him, light dawning, and punched his arm not all that gently. 'You knew! You knew all along what was wrong with him! You are such a rat!'

But Tom was chuckling and looking totally unrepentant. 'Why? I thought he deserved you.'

'Did you now? And what did I do to deserve him? Well, I'm glad you think it's so funny,' she added, trying to sound cross because he was cracking up by then, but his laughter was too infectious and she ended up in a fit of the giggles.

'Oh, well, it makes a change from doom and gloom, I suppose, and I think he's probably learned his lesson,' she said eventually, straightening up and wiping her eyes. 'I suppose we ought to go back to work. What time do you finish?'

He looked away, glancing down at the notes in his hand, all trace of laughter gone. 'Four. I've got an appointment.'

'An appointment?'

'Yeah, I'm having my eyes tested. I've been meaning to do it for a while but I haven't got round to it. I think I need glasses.'

He was avoiding her eye, and for no good

reason her heart gave a little thud. What wasn't he telling her?

'Oh. OK,' she said lightly. 'I just wondered if you wanted to pop round this evening for supper?'

'I haven't done the door yet.'

'That OK, I don't need the tools. Come anyway.'

'Are you sure? I can probably do the door before I come. It shouldn't take me long after I get back, it only needs a bit off the bottom.'

'Whatever. Come over as soon as you're ready,' she said without letting herself over-analyse it, and he nodded.

'That would be great. Maybe around seven, if I get done in time?'

'Seven's fine, but whenever. I'll make something quick.'

He left at four, walked down to the opticians and spent a few minutes pretending to look at the frames they had on offer.

What would they find? Anything? Nothing? Maybe he was worrying for no reason—

'Dr Stryker? I'm Julia Wilde, the optometrist. Would you like to come through?'

'Sure. Thank you.' His heart thumped, and he followed her into her room, sat down and told himself to relax. Ha-ha.

'So, I understand you've been having problems with your eyes recently? Can you tell me a bit more about that?'

'Well, it's nothing much, just a little difficulty with night vision,' he said, trying to keep a lid on his overactive imagination. 'It's probably just a vitamin deficiency or eye strain or too much time looking at screens...'

'Well, let's have a look, shall we?' she said, and started with a standard sight test which was no problem to him, tested his peripheral vision amongst other things, peered at his eyes with an ophthalmoscope, scanned and photographed the back of each eye in turn, and finally sat back.

'So what's the verdict? Do I need glasses?'

'No, your visual acuity is excellent, but your peripheral vision is a little restricted in places, and I think you might have a slight problem with your retinas. I can't be sure, so I'd like to refer you for further investigations, if that's OK,' she told him, her face carefully blank, and he felt his heart thud against his ribs.

'What kind of problem?' he asked, and as she turned the screen so he could see the images she'd taken, his blood ran cold.

'These are the retinal photographs, and as you can see there are a few tiny dots around the edges in both eyes, here and here, for example,' she said, pointing with her finger at the screen.

He shut his eyes for a second, then looked again, but the dots were still there, and his heart started to pound.

'That's... That's RP. Retinitis pigmentosa.'

'Let's not jump to conclusions. There are all sorts of things it could be and there are very few dots. They could be tiny bleeds, I don't know, which is why I want to refer you to the retina clinic at the hospital, because they have access to much better equipment than I do. They can do many more sophisticated tests that may be able to give you a more definitive diagnosis. Is there any history of night blindness in your family? Any parents or grandparents, uncles, aunts—anyone like that?'

He shook his head, his mind numb. 'No. No, I don't think so. I'm not sure. I'd have to ask.'

'Well, I don't want you to worry because

it could be nothing serious, but you do need a referral to get a proper diagnosis. I'll send it through now and you should hear within a few days. In the meantime keep a note of any times you find it harder to see, so we can work out if there's a pattern there. Do you have sunglasses?'

'Uh—yes. Yes, I do. They're polarised.'

'Good. Wear them whenever you're outside, preferably with orange filters to cut out blue light, just to protect your retinas as much as possible until we know what's going on.'

'Orange filters. OK. So, how long will it take before I'm seen?'

'It should be within a couple of weeks, but there's a bit of a backlog at the moment so it may take longer. But don't worry. As I say, it may not be anything serious at all.'

Don't worry? She must be dreaming.

He thanked her, walked out on autopilot, stumbled down to the sea front and sat on a bench and stared out across the water.

If it was RP, there was a good chance—or a very bad chance, to be more precise—that his vision would continue to deteriorate until at some time in the future he could be blind.

Blind! Unable to see his way around, unable to drive, to work—unable to have children for fear of passing it on because RP was hereditary?

And—when? Two years? Ten? Twenty?

He couldn't breathe properly because his chest felt so tight, and his heart was racing. He felt sick, sweat breaking out all over his body, and everything started to go black.

A panic attack. He was having a panic attack.

Breathe...

He cupped his hands over his mouth so he rebreathed his air, slowing down the intake of oxygen, telling himself to relax, to be calm, it was all right. It could be nothing. Maybe he was wrong. And gradually his heart slowed, his breathing sorted itself out and he felt the tension drain out of him and leave him trembling with exhaustion.

Why? Why would that happen?

Because this was different.

Everything else in life he'd had some control over, but not this. Not the possibility of going blind. He was totally unprepared for it, even though RP had been on his list of maybes. He'd dismissed it, though. It was so unlikely and there was no family history that he could think of. Surely, if it was RP, there would be.

So maybe it was something else? Something temporary, transient. Something treatable. Something less sinister.

Although nobody died of RP. It just slowly robbed you of your sight, over months and years and maybe decades, the edges of your vision creeping in until, if you were unlucky, almost nothing was left.

I don't want to go blind!

He got stiffly to his feet and walked home, went in through his sticking front door, shut it behind him and slid down it as if his strings were cut, his mind numb.

His phone rang, and he stared at the screen. Laura—and he'd had a missed call from her as well.

How could he talk to her? He couldn't tell her. He'd have to brush her off with some excuse. Heaven knows what, but he couldn't ignore her so he took a deep breath and answered.

'Hi. Sorry I missed your call, I was a bit tied up earlier.'

'That's OK. How did you get on? Are you going to have to wear sexy glasses?'

He laughed, but it came out like a strangled croak. 'No glasses,' he said. Nothing that simple. What on earth could he say? It was just a possibility, one of a host of things that could be wrong, and the last thing he wanted to do was to worry her. And no way could he cope with sympathy.

So he lied.

'Look, I'm in the middle of something—I'm doing some research for a paper and I really need to finish it. Do you mind if we give tonight a miss?'

'Oh—no, that's fine. Sure.'

Damn. She sounded wounded, but there was nothing he could do about it because he just wasn't ready to face her. Not ready to face anyone except maybe his parents, and possibly not even them.

'I'm sorry,' he said gently, and she murmured something and hung up, and he dropped the phone onto the floor and stared blankly at the wall opposite.

Oh, Laura… He wanted nothing more than to go round to her house and blurt it all out, but he couldn't. It wasn't fair, and it wasn't time. It wasn't as if he knew anything concrete yet. It was just a possibility. And anyway, even if it wasn't, how could he put all that on her when their relationship, if you could call it that, was so new and so fresh?

Emotion swamped him, and he buried his head in his hands and choked down a sob.

No! He was *not* going to do this! He wasn't going to give in to self-pity, not at this point. He didn't even know for sure, yet.

There'd be plenty of time to wallow in it later if it came to that, and then, once he'd had his referral appointment and been diagnosed and actually knew what was going on, then he'd talk to her. Maybe.

In the meantime he'd keep it to himself, and maybe find out a little bit more about his family history. And hopefully he'd draw a blank.

But he was twitchy, restless, and right now he needed to do something physical. He got out Laura's tools, yanked the door open and started work.

* * *

Something was wrong.

He didn't sound like himself at all. Had the optometrist found something sinister?

It could be any one of all sorts of things, but it was too much of a coincidence that he was suddenly weird immediately after the appointment, and it worried her.

She'd already made a salad and baked some tandoori chicken breasts and a part-baked garlic bread baton that she found in the freezer. She left them in the oven to keep warm, put the salad back in the fridge, gave Millie a biscuit and drove round to his house.

He was working on the door—not a paper at all, but the door, attacking it with the rasp as if his life depended on it.

Or his sanity?

He glanced up at her as she shut the car door, his face taut and unforgiving.

'I said I was busy.'

'You said you were doing research for a paper. I didn't realise it was for a DIY magazine.'

He put the rasp down. Well, no, he threw it

down, and got to his feet with a growl. 'What do you want, Laura?'

She walked up to him and stood on the doorstep. No way was she going to back down, not when he was in this state. 'I want you to talk to me,' she said gently. 'What did they say?'

'Who?'

'The optometrist.'

He looked away, and she could see a muscle jumping in his jaw. 'Nothing.'

'That's rubbish.' She stepped over the heap of sawdust and wood shavings and looked at the door, shook her head in disbelief and closed it behind her. 'What on earth are you doing to this poor door?'

'Making it fit.'

'No, you're destroying it,' she said, and picked up the rasp, threw it back in the bag with the other tools and shook her head again.

'I made supper. I'm guessing you haven't eaten.'

'I'm not hungry.'

'Tom, stop it. I don't know what's going on, but I'm not leaving you like this. Come on, come home with me and let's have something to eat and talk it over.'

'I don't need to talk to you.'

'Well, who are you going to talk to?' She took him by the shoulders and stared into his eyes. 'I'm the only person here that you know, and you look to me like a man who needs a friendly shoulder right now, so here it is. No strings.'

She saw him swallow, saw a flicker of emotion in those deep slate eyes before he blanked it. 'Laura, I'm fine—'

'Don't lie, Tom. You told me you never lie to me, so don't start now. What did they say?'

He held out for several seconds, but she didn't back down, and eventually his shoulders dropped.

'I've got a referral,' he said.

'Because?'

'She found something. Spots. Dark spots, round the edge of my retinas. And my peripheral vision is patchy.'

She closed her eyes briefly, drew in a slow breath and let it go. 'There could be all sorts of reasons for that,' she said, but there was only one she could think of, and one of the first symptoms was night blindness. And he'd tripped over the kerb in the dark the night they'd gone for dinner, said he hadn't seen it. And if he had retinitis pigmentosa...

'Such as?'

She looked up at him, and his face was taut with suppressed emotion. Oh, Tom...

She dropped her hands and looked away. 'I don't know. I haven't seen the scans, I'm not a specialist, I don't know anything about eyes.'

'Yes, you do. You know enough to know that's the typical presentation of RP, and if I have that it's going to get worse and worse until eventually I might lose much or all of my sight, and there isn't a damn thing anyone can do about it.'

'But you don't know that you've got it until you've had the referral. You're jumping the gun. Come on, get in the car and come back with me before the chicken gets stone cold. We can talk about it there.'

'I don't want to talk about it.'

She smiled at him and kissed his cheek, swallowing down the tears that were threatening in the wings. 'That's fine, you don't have to. We can talk about something else. You can tell me why you left London.'

He gave a huff of humourless laughter. 'Yeah, because that's so much better.'

'I wouldn't know. I know nothing about it, so why don't you tell me?'

'Why should I? Just because we were friends once doesn't mean I want to spill my guts to you. I don't want to talk about it.'

'So? I didn't want to talk about my mother last night, but I did. And you know what? It helped. So shut up whinging, get in the car and let's at least eat before we both die of hunger.'

'I'm fixing the door.'

'No,' she said firmly, 'you're not. You're trashing it, Tom. You're not in the right frame of mind to tackle it properly, and you need to leave it alone while there's still a door left to fix. Tomorrow's another day. Come on.'

She opened the door and stood there, and he shook his head, gave a short huff of what might just have been laughter and picked up his keys.

'You're a nag, do you know that?'

'Yup. Come on.'

He shut the door, got into her car and sat,

arms folded, staring straight ahead while she drove him back to her house.

He followed her in, and Millie greeted him at the door like a long-lost friend, and she saw his face contort a little. 'Hello, sweetie,' he murmured, and bent down to stroke her. 'You're a good girl, aren't you?'

'She is a good girl. She's also a flirt. Come on through to the kitchen. It's all ready.'

She headed for the kitchen and then realised he wasn't following her, so she went back and found him standing open-mouthed in the archway that led to the study.

Grumps had had it fitted floor to ceiling with beautiful bespoke library shelves, all of them full, and everyone was stunned by it so she wasn't surprised to see that Tom was, too. She was just a little surprised by what he said.

'This is incredible,' he murmured, his voice sounding slightly awed. 'I've never seen so many books in one house before—well, apart from ours. My mother's an antiquarian bookseller and my father's an avid reader, so home's always naturally been overrun with books, but not like this. This is…'

He lifted a hand towards the spine of one of the oldest books, his hovering fingers an inch away, almost reverently. 'Have you had them valued?'

'No. I haven't done anything with anything. I don't even know where to start. He used to say there were ten thousand of them, but I have no idea and life's too short to count them. And anyway, they're his. It's where I sit when I want to be near him, which is one reason I liked working in the library at college, and frankly I don't really want to touch them. I love it like it is.'

'You should get an insurance valuation.'

'Maybe. I suppose some of them might be worth something, not that I'll sell them. There are some rare first editions, apparently, but I have no idea where. He showed them to me ages ago, when I was at uni, and told me one day they'd be mine. To be honest I wasn't that interested back then, it was too far in the future to think about, and then it was too late.'

She sucked in a breath and slid open the pocket door that led to the dining room. 'Come on, the chicken will be freezing. Let's eat.'

* * *

Tom pushed away his plate and smiled at her ruefully. 'That was lovely. Thank you. I'm sorry I was such a grump.'

'Don't worry about it. You had a good excuse. Would you like a coffee?'

'That would be great, thanks. It's been quite a day.'

'So it seems. What made you make the appointment?'

He shrugged. 'What you said after we'd had dinner back in February, when I tripped over the kerb. It wasn't the first time I'd stumbled in the dark, and it wasn't the last. It just made me think I should get it checked out. I'd been telling myself for ages it was nothing, just eye strain or whatever, but I was in denial.'

'You still don't know for sure,' she reminded him gently, and he nodded.

'Yeah, you're right. I don't. My grandmother used to say something about not borrowing trouble. Maybe she had a point.'

She spooned ground coffee into the cafetière and poured boiling water on it, and he sat at the table with Millie's head on his lap, stroking her and tugging her ears gently and mur-

muring sweet nothings while she gazed up at him adoringly and Laura poured the coffee and tried not to cry.

'Millie, you're a hussy. Let's go and sit in the garden. She loves fossicking around in the undergrowth. I think it should be warm enough. Do you want me to put the outside lights on?'

'No, you're fine,' he said, but then he missed the step in the fading light and she felt a jolt of fear for him. Oh, Tom…

'Are you OK? I'm sorry, I should have warned you about the step. Let me put the lights on.'

'No, leave it. I'll be better in a few minutes.'

'Are you sure?'

'Yes, I'm sure. Don't fuss. It's not that bad.'

She wasn't sure if he was telling her the truth, but there was something lovely about sitting there with the twilight wrapped around them like a cloak, oddly intimate and comforting. She turned to look at him in the semi-darkness.

He was motionless, staring out across the garden, his face set in stone, and she felt a pang of guilt. She should have put the lights on, but maybe he'd be more likely to talk to her if they couldn't see so well.

'Tom?'

He turned his head, his mouth tilting a little into a smile that broke her heart. 'You're right. It's nice out here. Peaceful.'

'It is. It was my grandfather's favourite place. We sat here a lot, especially after his stroke when he couldn't get out any more.'

'Couldn't he use a mobility scooter?'

'No, he couldn't. Not with Millie. She wouldn't have been able to guide him.'

'Guide him?'

'Yes—he was blind. I thought you knew that? He went blind years ago.'

He stared at her blankly. 'I didn't know he was blind. All those books. What a waste. And Millie?' He looked down at her head on his lap, his hand resting gently on it, stroking her lovingly. 'Millie's a guide dog?'

'Yes. Well, she was. She's ten now, and they retire at about nine or ten, so he was allowed to keep her after he had his stroke because I was with him, and then when he died I said I'd keep her with me and they were OK with it because I'd known her for years and she's happy with me.'

She could see the shock on his face still as he took all that in. 'How did he cope? When he went blind? Was it sudden?'

She shrugged. 'No, it wasn't. He had macular degeneration and it was so gradual at first that he had time to adapt.'

'Like RP,' he said slowly, and she felt her heart pick up.

'A bit, but it progressed quite rapidly and because he'd had the odd mini stroke he wasn't able to have the injections they wanted to give him, so by the end he couldn't see anything well enough to identify it really.'

'And Millie? When did he get her?'

'While I was at uni, just before my final year.'

'You didn't tell me that.'

She smiled. 'We weren't really talking much then. Anyway, he went on the waiting list for a guide dog once he couldn't manage any more, and he got Millie six months later, when she was two, and they bonded instantly. She took him everywhere safely for nearly seven years, bless her. Unlike RP where it's a long time before the central vision goes, if it ever does, he'd lost his central vision completely by the time he got her, but he still retained some peripheral vision which helped him with navigation but just meant he couldn't read or see what he was doing. At least with RP you can still see to read facial expressions almost to the end, but he'd lost that long ago.'

He grunted. 'For someone who knows nothing about eyes, you seem to know a lot about it.'

'Not really.'

'You do. I reckon you knew exactly what it was when I told you what the optometrist said.'

She felt a twinge of guilt. 'No. I knew what it *could* be, but I didn't want to compound it with an uneducated off-the-cuff diagnosis. I wanted to support you, to stop you worrying overly before you needed to, because it could be something else, Tom. You still don't know for sure.'

She heard him huff dismissively. 'I do know, and so do you, and anything less than facing that reality is clutching at straws. And I don't need your support. I'm fine.'

She let out a tiny, shaky sigh. 'I'm sorry,'

she said softly. 'You're right, and anyway, it's none of my business.'

'I didn't say that.'

'You didn't need to, Tom. I'm just presuming on our old friendship, and I probably shouldn't do that. Like last night. I was a bit judgemental about the way you were at uni. That wasn't any of my business, either.'

She saw his mouth tilt into a wry smile. 'I don't know. I pretty much made it your business. And yes, you were, but I can see why now, with your mother being like that. For the record, I did have a couple of short relationships while we were there.'

'You did? When?'

'Early on. But they wanted more than I did, and a few dates in they were leaving a tooth-brush next to mine and spare underwear in the drawer. It was the thin end of the wedge, angling for moving in, and there was no way I wanted that, not at that point in my life.'

'Other people did. Lots of them coupled up.'

'I know, and most of them uncoupled again over the course of the next five years with all sorts of emotional fallout, and of the ones that didn't most of them have split up by now. Life's tough as a junior doctor, and I just didn't want the hassle. I was too young to settle down, I knew I had years ahead of me of moving from job to job in different cities, which is incredibly disruptive. I wasn't ready.'

She blew on her coffee and eyed him over the top of it. 'That was years ago, though, so what's your excuse now?'

She searched his eyes, but she couldn't read them any longer in the dim light, and then he looked away and shrugged. 'I've come close. Only the once, but that was enough, and it was definitely a mistake.' He hesitated, shrugged again, and looked back at her. 'Still, it's done now and I've moved on.'

Done now? 'Is that why you left London? Not that you have to tell me...'

He smiled again and nodded slowly. 'Yeah. It was one of the reasons. Karen was working in the same hospital as me and she'd moved in with me, we'd talked about buying a house together, so I put my flat on the market and my boss wanted to buy it because it was so handy, so it was ideal. And by then I wanted to get out of London, move somewhere rural, somewhere cleaner and less crowded, somewhere like this, but I was working crazy hours, so was she, so we didn't do anything about finding new jobs. To be honest we hardly saw each other for weeks, so we just didn't have time. And then at the end of January, after my seventh fourteen-hour night shift in a row, I went home and found Karen in bed with him. Our bed.'

'With your *boss*?'

'Yeah. The one buying my flat because it was so handy. A bit like your mother and your boyfriend. People you trust—only you can't. I guess we both learned that the hard way.'

'Oh, Tom.' She shook her head in disbelief. 'That's awful.'

'Yeah. And even then she didn't tell me the truth. She tried to explain it away by saying he'd missed the last train so she'd let him stay over.'

'In your bed?'

'Well, exactly. We had a sofa bed in the lounge, he could have slept on that, but it was all lies. It had probably been going on behind my back for months. I think they'd planned the whole thing, including him buying the flat.'

'So what did you do?'

He gave a bitter little laugh that made her ache for him. 'I told him if he upped his offer he could have the flat immediately with all its contents, including Karen, and I handed in my notice and told him I'd be taking payment for all my holiday and time in lieu and leaving at the end of March with a damn good reference, and if he didn't want the Board to know what he'd been doing he'd better make sure it happened. Then I looked for jobs, found this one, phoned and spoke to James because I'd just missed the deadline, zapped him over my CV and he tacked me on the interview list. The rest, as they say, is history.'

She tried to smile, but she was still shocked at how his girlfriend had treated him. 'How could she? How could she do that to you—to anyone?'

He shrugged again. 'We were never there at the same time, our sex life was practically non-existent, and she told me she was lonely. But apparently I was better in bed, if it was any consolation.'

Laura felt her eyes widen. 'She actually said that to you?'

He nodded. 'Yes. She actually said that. I

told her it was her loss. We haven't spoken since.'

'Oh, Tom. I'm so sorry. How could she do that to you? Didn't she care about you at all?'

'Apparently not. Turns out I was no more than a meal ticket, and Adrian was paid more. So how about you? How come you're still alone?' he asked, and she swallowed.

'I wasn't. Not until I moved back here. I had a boyfriend—Pete. I was living with him, and Grumps had had a couple of very minor strokes, but then he had another at the beginning of March and couldn't really look after himself, and I couldn't bear the thought of him going into a home. He would have found it so disorientating without his sight, and he'd taken such good care of me when I needed him, and it would have meant him losing Millie which would have broken his heart, so I chucked in my job in Nottingham and came here to look after him, and that was the end of it for me and Pete. I started doing a few locum shifts which was a bit of a lifeline, and I got to spend lots of time with Grumps, and I wouldn't change a second of it. Well, except the end, of course. That was…'

She felt his hand on her shoulder, warm and gentle, a little squeeze for comfort, and she laid her fingers over his and he curled them into his palm and held them.

'Gosh, we're cheery tonight,' she said after a long moment, and gave herself a little mental shake. 'Tell me about your mother. She sounds interesting.'

He chuckled softly, the sound wrapping round her in the darkness. 'Where do I start? She's a great mum in a lot of ways, but she's a bit of a workaholic and she spends a huge amount of time in her bookshop researching stuff and repairing old books. She's very talented and very interesting. I think she and your grandfather would have got on well.'

'Oh, I'm sure they would, from the sound of that. He knew all the books on his shelves, all ten thousand of them or whatever. If I wanted to know anything, he knew exactly where to find the answer. He had a mind like a steel trap.'

'It must run in the family,' he said, and she could hear the smile in his voice. He gave her hand another squeeze.

'It's getting late. I ought to go home,' he said

softly, and she nodded, but for a long time neither of them moved, and his thumb was stroking slowly over the back of her hand, sending tingles along her arm.

She eased her hand away and stood up, gathering up their cups and putting them on the tray, and he picked it up and followed her in. She heard a clatter and he swore, and she flicked the light on and turned to take the tray.

'Are you OK?'

'Yeah, I missed the step. Again. My night vision's apparently total rubbish. Ignore me.'

Ignore him? When he was poised on the brink of a precipice with his sight hanging in the balance? Unlikely.

She took the tray from him, put it down and headed towards the front door, switching on the table lamp on the old carved chest in the hall.

He paused by the door, his face bathed in the gentle light, staring down into her eyes. 'Thank you for feeding me, it was really tasty. And for the tools. I'll let you have them back as soon as I'm done, and I promise I'll do the door properly this time.'

She smiled. 'No hurry,' she said, and went up on tiptoe to kiss him goodbye.

Error? Or the best thing she'd done in ages?

Because it wasn't just a kiss, a friendly peck on the cheek, even though it was meant to be.

For some reason it morphed into an invitation, and he turned his head a fraction, his lips warm and firm and supple as they found hers, and with a soft sigh he cradled her head in his hands, settled his mouth on hers and kissed her.

Really kissed her, his lips slow and gentle, gradually deepening the kiss until her legs turned to jelly and she could hardly stand.

Then he lifted his head and stared down into her eyes.

'I'm not looking for a relationship, Laura, you have to know that.'

'I know that. Nor am I.'

'So where's this going?' he asked softly, and she held his eyes, reading the need, the tenderness, the restraint. And the fear, lurking in the background. She couldn't let him go. Not tonight, and maybe not ever.

She smiled. 'That depends on the contents of your wallet.'

He gave a surprised little laugh, and his eyes crinkled and lit up. 'You're after my money?' And then he stopped teasing her, the smile changing again, back to tender. Back to sexy.

'Don't worry. I didn't trust myself around you. My wallet's ready for this.'

She swallowed, her heart hammering in her chest, her body aching for his. She opened her mouth to speak, but nothing came out except a soft sigh of relief as her lips tilted into a smile.

She held out her hand, and he took it, letting her lead him into her bedroom.

'Millie, no, in your bed,' she said, and Millie turned and padded back towards the kitchen. By the time she'd closed the door he'd turned on the bedside light, and he held out his hand to her.

'Come here. You're far too far away.'

She walked up to him, reaching for the buttons on his shirt, trailing her lips over his skin as she went. She touched her tongue to his nipples, one after the other, then blew softly, feeling the change in texture as they tightened in response.

'You do know you're killing me?' he said calmly, although he wasn't calm. She could feel his heart against her mouth, just the other side of his ribs, the solid thud reassuringly strong. She lifted her head and looked up into his beautiful eyes. The eyes that could be going blind....

'I want you,' she said softly, and he groaned and hauled her into his arms, ditching his restraint.

Their clothes were in the way, so they ditched them, too, coming together skin to skin with gasps and sighs. She could feel the tension in him, the heat of his skin, the hard jut of his erection against her abdomen as he kissed her again, his tongue delving, thrusting, his teeth taking gentle bites of her lips as he pulled away to look down at her body.

'So soft,' he murmured, his hands cradling her breasts, lifting them to his lips, suckling her nipples deeply into his mouth in turn and sending sharp arrows of need deep into her body.

She let out a shuddering sigh and he pulled away, groping for his wallet. Then he was back, tugging the duvet out of the way and tumbling them onto the bed in a tangle of arms and legs, his hands and mouth roaming freely all over her until she was ready to scream with frustration.

'Please…'

And he was there, their bodies merged, moving to a rhythm as old as time. She felt him tense, felt her body explode with sensation as it convulsed around him and then was still, felt the racing of his heart against her, the heave of his chest as he sucked in air, the aftershocks that took her breath away, and then he stroked the hair away from her eyes and kissed her, and nothing had ever felt so right.

CHAPTER SIX

'I SHOULD GO HOME.'

She stirred, her head shifting on his shoulder as she turned it to look at him, her eyes soft and sleepy.

'You probably should. I'm on an early shift tomorrow, and I need to walk Millie before I go, which means a hideously early start.'

'What happens to her while you're at work?'

'She has a dog walker—she calls herself the Fairy Dogmother, and she's been walking her for years. She takes her out into the country and lets her off to play, which Grumps couldn't do, and she's been really brilliant. She walks her at some point every day, even if I'm around, because my shifts are so random that I never know when I'll be needed so it gives me flexibility. I'd be lost without her, and so would Millie. She loves her to bits.'

'She loves everyone, doesn't she? She certainly smiles at me.'

'She does. She's a proper softie. Grumps adored her.'

She shifted closer, turning his face towards her and touching her lips to his, and his body stirred.

How could he still want her so much? They'd just had mind-blowing sex—what, half an hour ago? Maybe less. And he wanted her again.

'Uh-uh, you need your sleep,' he mumbled against her lips, and eased away, dropping a kiss on her nose as he threw back the duvet and rolled away from her and stood up, scouring the room for his clothes. He plucked his jersey shorts off the back of a chair, his jeans off the floor, his shirt from the end of the bed. He had no idea where his socks were.

Ah. There. Snuggled up with her bra. He pulled them on, slid his feet into his shoes and stood up, and she wriggled up the bed and sat up, pulling the duvet up under her arms—but not before he'd watched her breasts jostling gently with the movement.

He groaned inwardly at his body's enthusiastic response, scooped up his wallet and leant over to kiss her.

'Thanks again for supper and the tools. I'll

see you tomorrow. I don't start till midday, so I'll see if I can get the door fixed before then.'

'No rush.'

He chuckled. 'There is if I'm not going to break the glass. It's still sticking a bit despite my worst efforts. Don't move, I'll let myself out.'

'Will you be OK in the dark? Can you see to get home or do you want a lift?'

'I've got a torch on my phone. I'll be fine.'

He dropped another kiss on her soft, yielding and oh-so-tempting lips, and walked away while he still could.

How can I want her so much?

Millie came to the door to see him out, her smile bringing a lump to his throat. Would he have a dog like her one day, a dog to guide him and keep him safer? Would he need one?

Don't jump the gun.

He gave her a little fuss then let himself out, and his movement triggered the outside light. Another thing he could do with at his new house, he thought, and he switched on his torch and walked carefully home, wishing he'd had the foresight to leave the porch light on.

No matter. He used the torch to find the key-hole, and opened the front door with slightly less than the usual fight.

Poor thing. She was right, he'd trashed it. Thank God she'd come when she had and stopped him. He'd fix it first thing.

He shut the door with his foot, got himself a glass of water and headed up to bed.

She hardly saw Tom the next day—just enough to share a smile and in his case a wicked little wink before he was plunged back into the fray in Resus, shortly after what should have been her mid-afternoon break. Not that she'd had lunch either—

'Go and grab a coffee while it's not insane,' James said, appearing at her elbow, so she put down the set of notes she'd just picked up and headed down to the café before he changed his mind.

She wasn't sure if Tom would have had lunch before he'd left for work. Probably, but just in case she picked up a wrapped muffin that would keep for a day or two, and a coffee which definitely wouldn't but might keep him going a bit longer, and took them and her own coffee and almond croissant out into the park to sit in the sun for five minutes.

'Hi.'

She glanced up and saw Livvy Hunter coming towards her, her subtle baby bump now visible under her scrubs, and she waved at the chair opposite.

'Hi there. Come and join me. I'm just grabbing some vitamin D while the going's good.'

Livvy sat down and eyed Tom's muffin.

'Two cakes? Isn't that getting a bit much?'

Damn. 'Yeah, they're not both for me. One's for Tom.'

Livvy's eyes narrowed slightly, and Laura could swear there were little lumps under her hair where her antennae had pricked up. Time for some damage limitation.

'He's been in Resus since he arrived, and he was just coming out and the red phone rang again, so I thought I'd take him back something as I was here.'

'Yeah, right,' Livvy said, tipping her head on one side. 'You look different.'

So much for damage limitation. She held her friend's eyes with difficulty. 'Different?'

'Yes. As in—well, I don't know. Loved up?'

She lost the battle and glanced down, tearing her croissant into bite-sized bits. 'Why would I look loved up?'

'I don't know. You tell me.'

No way on earth.

'I'm just happy. Happy that the weather's better and the sun's out, happy that I'm finally having some lunch, happy that you're doing so well with your pregnancy—that's all. Just happy.' She could feel Livvy's eyes on her, and looked up and met them. 'Is that a problem?'

'Of course it's not a problem. It's *lovely* to see you happy, after all you've been through. It's just...'

'Just what?'

'Just—a bit coincidental.'

She shrugged. 'Maybe. But that's all it is. Anyway, what are you doing here on your day off?'

'I've just had my twenty-week scan,' Livvy said, and Laura didn't need to ask. Her smile said it all.

'Did you get a picture?'

'Of course.' She pulled the envelope out of

her bag, opened it and passed Laura a slightly grainy image of her baby's face.

'Oh, that's just so magical! So, everything's OK?'

'Yes, everything's absolutely fine. Matt was with me, and we both welled up a bit. He didn't think we would ever be able to have a baby after my cancer treatment, and I certainly didn't, and it took a while for me to get pregnant, but now—I'm actually starting to believe it, and Amber and Charlie are getting excited, and it's all good.'

Laura felt her own eyes welling. 'Oh, Livvy, I'm so happy for you that it's all working out so well. That's such great news. Do you know what it is?'

'Yes. She's a girl. Amber's going to be ecstatic. She was desperate for a little sister.' There was a tiny pause, and then Livvy added softly, 'We're going to call her Juliet, after Matt's first wife. Only her middle name, but we just wanted her to be a part of this, because she'll always be a part of our family.'

Now Laura really was welling up, and she sniffed and blinked and squeezed Libby's hand. 'Oh, Livvy. Juliet's a lovely name, and what a beautiful way to remember her.'

'We thought so. Can I steal a bit of your croissant?'

Laura laughed and pushed the plate towards her. 'Have the rest of it. I need to get back.'

She did. Her pager bleeped in her pocket, and she pulled it out and read the screen.

'Resus. Joy. See you tomorrow.'

She leant over and kissed Livvy's cheek, and grabbing Tom's coffee and muffin she headed back via the park, going in through the staff door into the back entrance of the ED.

She parked the coffee and muffin behind the work station and went into Resus where Ryan McKenna was just starting to brief the team.

She smiled back at Tom as she passed him, and went up to Ryan. 'So what have we got?'

It was gone midnight before he got home after his twelve-hour shift, and of course he'd forgotten to put the porch light on when he'd left at midday in blazing sunshine.

Damn. He really, really needed to get an outside light with a motion sensor so he could find his way to the door after the street lights were out.

And just to underline the necessity, he misjudged the step again and smacked his hand against the doorframe, digging the keys into his palm. Swearing fluently, he pulled his phone out of his pocket and turned on the torch, got the key in the lock and went in and studied his hand in the light.

It hadn't broken the skin, luckily, but it still hurt and his knuckles were bruised. Stupid, but at least the front door opened and shut now. Small mercies.

He threw the keys down on the hall table in disgust and went through to the kitchen. All he'd had all day apart from a couple of glasses of water was a coffee and a big fat muffin Laura had brought him back from the Park Café after her break. He'd finally got to it at five, when the coffee was well and truly cold, but at least nobody had stolen the muffin.

He opened the fridge and studied the contents. Nothing instant, nothing he could ping in the microwave, but he did have cheese, and he had some salad, so he made himself a massive cheese salad sandwich, squirted mayo into it and dropped into the sofa, turning on the television and scrolling down the guide without any real interest.

He was too tired to bother, too strung out after his full-on shift to sleep, and always in the background was the niggling worry of his eyes. He'd had the day from hell, and all he really wanted was to crawl into bed with Laura and hide from the world.

Could he do that? Would it be fair or reasonable?

Absolutely not, not in any way, but he pulled his phone out and saw a message from her.

'Call me when you finish, if you want to?'

He wanted, he definitely wanted, but it wasn't fair.

In which case, she shouldn't have said it.

He cracked and called her, and she sounded warm and sleepy and he felt instantly guilty. 'Damn. I'm sorry, I've woken you up.'

'Not really, I was only dozing. I was expecting your call. How was it?'

'Hell, frankly. What did you expect? It's Saturday night.'

'Want to come round?'

Did he ever. 'I need a shower. Can you wait?'

'Of course I can wait. I've got a day off to-morrow.'

Twenty minutes later he was walking into her arms, and it felt so good he could have cried.

He didn't. He took her back to bed, wrapped her in his arms and fell asleep instantly.

Laura woke with a crick in her neck, a heavy arm draped over her waist and a warm body curled around her back. She shifted her head, tugged the pillow under it better and felt him stir against her.

'Morning,' she murmured, and he grunted.

'Time is it?' he mumbled, almost inaudibly, and she felt herself smile.

'Six-thirty.'

'Umph.'

She wriggled out from under his arm and went to the bathroom, and when she came back he slung his arm over her and she felt a warm hand curl around her breast. 'Mmm,' he said. 'Feels good.'

She half expected him to fall asleep again, but he didn't, he went to the bathroom and then came back smelling of toothpaste and warm, sleepy man, his body snuggling more firmly against hers. She felt him start to nibble her shoulder, his thumb sweeping idly over her nipple, his hips pressing gently against her bottom. 'So good.'

She turned in his arms and he nudged one leg between hers and sighed. 'Mmm. That's nice.'

His mouth found hers, coaxing, nibbling, his hands slow and lazy and warm, and then he rolled away, rummaged on the floor and came back with a smile and a little foil packet.

She took it from him, tipped him onto his back and took control.

His eyes scrunched shut. 'You're torturing me.'

'Mmm. It's fun.'

She straddled him, her hands on his shoulders, pinning him to the bed while she rocked slowly against him until he lost it and took over, and what had started as warm and lazy and tender turned into hot and hard and fast as he drove them over the edge into a maelstrom of sensation that robbed her of breath, of thought, of reason.

And then he rolled to his side, taking her with him, and they lay face to face, their heads together, their breath mingling as it slowed and their bodies recovered.

'Wow.' He laughed softly and stroked her face with a gentle hand. 'That was something else. Maybe I should stay over more often.'

He kissed her tenderly, then rolled away and got out of bed, heading for the bathroom again, and she lay on her back staring at the ceiling and wondering how she'd let herself fall in love with him so hard, so far, so fast.

She needed to go on the Pill again if this was going to keep happening, because one of these days his wallet wouldn't come up with the goods and the last thing either of them needed was an unplanned pregnancy.

Assuming it did keep happening, because he'd told her in no uncertain terms that they weren't going anywhere, so there was no point building dreams on it. He was just in a bad place because of his eyes, and he needed the comfort and distraction she could provide. Nothing more. He'd probably still shut her out when the going got tougher.

He was gone a while, and when he came back it was with two mugs and a happy dog, who jumped up on the end of the bed and left wet pawprints on the duvet cover.

'Oh, Millie, you'll get me in trouble,' he said, getting back into bed and propping himself up. 'Sorry, somebody wanted to go out but I thought I'd wiped her feet better than that. It must have rained in the night.'

'It doesn't matter, it happens all the time, it'll wash. What's in the mugs?'

'Tea.'

She sat herself up and he passed it to her, and she frowned as she took it. 'What have you done to your hand?'

'Oh, that,' he said, sounding cross and frustrated. 'I tripped over the front doorstep last night in the dark and smacked it into the doorframe. I dug the keys into the palm, as well, so it's a bit tetchy today. You'd think by now I'd know there's a step there. Apparently not.'

She put her tea down and picked up his hand, turning it over to reveal a dark purple bruise spreading over his palm, to match the purple across two of his knuckles.

'Wiggle your fingers?'

'It's not broken, Laura. It's fine. It's just a bit sore if you poke it like that!' he added, his voice rising slightly in pitch as he snatched it back.

'Hmm. You ought to be more careful.'

'No, I ought to have an outside light that sees me coming and turns on automatically instead of the porch light that I never remember to put on, but that means an electrician.'

'Or you could have a dusk-to-dawn bulb in the porch light. You leave it on all the time, and it comes on when it gets dark and goes off when it gets light.'

'There's such a thing?'

'Yup.' And it was something she could do for him to make life easier and safer. Goodness knows there was precious little else she could do to help him. She picked up her phone, typed in her search, and with a couple of clicks she put her phone down and smiled at him. 'Sorted. I've ordered you one. It'll be here in a couple of days.'

He grinned at her. 'You're a star. I didn't even know they existed.' He leant over and kissed her, then settled back against the pillows with a contented sigh. 'So, I start work at twelve again today. Do you have any plans for the morning?'

'No. Well, walking Millie, but otherwise no. Why?'

'I just thought we could go out for breakfast.'

'Well, there's a lovely idea. Anywhere in mind?'

He shrugged. 'You're the local. You tell me.'

'They do a mean brunch at the Harbour Inn down by the river mouth. We can take Millie with us and sit outside if it stays sunny, and if not they allow dogs in the bar. Or there's a boutique hotel on the prom with a sea view and seats outside? That's closer if the weather stays OK.'

It did, and they went to the hotel and sat in the sunshine with Millie at their feet, wet and sandy from romping in the surf, and ate fat juicy BLT baps washed down with buckets of coffee before walking back to hers.

'I need to head straight off, really,' he said, and she nodded and went up on tiptoe and kissed him.

'I hope it's better than yesterday.'

He gave a short laugh and shook his head. 'I'm not holding my breath.' He brushed his bruised knuckles lightly over her cheek. 'Have a lovely day. I'll see you tomorrow. What time are you on?'

She wrinkled her nose. 'Six.'

'In which case I won't come over after my shift, because it'll just disturb us both, but I'll see you later. I'm on nine to nine tomorrow.'

'OK. And be careful when you get home. Or put the porch light on before you leave!'

He grinned. 'I will. You take care.'

He dropped another kiss on her lips, lingering for just a fraction, then got into his car and drove away, and she went inside with Millie, humming to herself as she pottered round the house, and then realised what Livvy had seen in her eyes.

Happiness—but she was deluding herself, playing happy families, and it was dangerous because it was based on nothing. He'd told her clearly that this was going nowhere, that he had nothing to offer her, that he wanted her to be free. It was the last thing she wanted, but if he was told for sure that he had RP, would he want her then, or would he try and drive her away?

She had no idea, but she'd do her damnedest

to support him, and if he wouldn't let her, well then he wouldn't. But for now she had him, and even if it only lasted a few weeks she'd take it, and just hope she'd survive when it all went wrong.

Time to toughen up.

She went into the bedroom, stripped the bed and held the bedding to her nose. It smelt of him, warm and musky and delicious, and it made her want to cry. She put it in the washing machine, shut the door firmly and took Millie for a walk.

Over the course of the next week they fell into a sort of pattern.

Sometimes they worked together, sometimes not, but usually they saw each other in the department at some point during the day. If they finished at a reasonable hour, they'd eat together. If one of them was held up, they wouldn't.

But almost always, they'd end up together at the end of the day, most often at Laura's because of Millie.

And Millie was besotted by him.

Laura was, too, but she was a bit more discreet than Millie, who lay at his feet or on the sofa at his side, eyes fixed on him adoringly or slightly glazed if he rested a hand on her and stroked her gently in the special way he seemed to have.

She could have been jealous of the dog, but she knew her turn would come later, when they'd go into her bedroom and close the door and his hands would be on her.

He didn't stay the night again, though, after that first time, partly because of their conflicting shift patterns, but also maybe because she suspected he didn't want it to become a habit, a custom, a way of drifting into something he didn't want. And always at the back of her mind was his comment about the girls who'd leave a toothbrush next to his, or underwear in his drawer, and the last thing she wanted was to make assumptions.

Like she had with Pete. She'd moved in with him, and just assumed he felt the same about her as she did about him. She'd expected him to understand when she had to drop everything and come home to look after Grumps, but he hadn't. He hadn't understood at all, and the first weekend she didn't go back, he turned up at his door with her things. All of them.

'You'll need these,' he said, and unloaded his car and drove away without a backward glance, leaving her in no doubt about how little she'd meant to him.

So she wasn't in a hurry to put herself in that position again, and neither was Tom after his experience with Karen, and adding his eyes into the mix just made it worse, but it didn't stop them making love at every opportunity, and it didn't stop her loving him even though she knew it was doomed to failure.

He was away the next weekend, visiting his parents, and she missed him ridiculously. He didn't ring, and even when she knew he was back because she'd seen his car while she was walking Millie on Sunday evening, she still heard nothing from him. She had Monday off, so she didn't see him at work, and still he didn't ring her.

Why? Was he avoiding her? What had they told him? She could only guess, and her stomach was in knots.

* * *

The weekend with his parents had already been scheduled to fit in with their busy timetables, but as it turned out he almost wished it hadn't.

He drove up on Saturday morning, and they spent the rest of the day working on the garden while they talked, and on Sunday it rained so he showed them photos of the house. 'Just so you know what I've taken on,' he said with a rueful grin.

'Darling, you must be mad! I thought you wanted an easier life?' his mother said, handing the phone back, and he thought about what might be ahead of him and laughed. If you could call it that. He passed the phone to his father.

'Oh, dear. Did you realise it was that bad?' he said, scrolling through the photos, and Tom gave another hollow laugh.

'Not really, but it's getting better. At least the front door doesn't stick any more. I managed to borrow some tools from Laura—you probably won't remember her, I was at college with her.'

'I remember her name—you talked about her rather a lot,' his mother said pointedly.

'Well, we were good friends, so I would. Actually, you'd be really interested. She lived with her grandfather in Yoxburgh, and he's died and she's got all his books. They're amazing, and she really needs a valuation. I think she said there are ten thousand?'

'Good grief. Anything old?'

'Oh, yes. You'd be in heaven. There were some beautiful books, and she talked about some very old first editions.'

'Oh, I'd love to see them. Maybe when we come down to stay. So—are you together now?'

'No,' he said, maybe a little too hastily. 'No, Mum, we're not, and certainly not so soon after Karen. I think I've learned my lesson. We're just friends, which is a miracle as I got the job she'd also applied for, but hey. That's life.'

And hers was infinitely more complicated since he'd rocked up, but there was nothing he could do about that—apart from not complicate it any further, which he was failing at miserably. And on the subject of failing miserably, he still hadn't asked them about family history, but he didn't want to worry them and he knew they weren't stupid. How to raise it?

He didn't need to, in the end, because his mother raised it quite by accident. 'So what time are you heading home, darling?' she asked. 'Are you staying for supper or will you want to head off? You don't want to drive in the dark, especially when it's raining. Well, I wouldn't.'

And then it dawned on him that she'd never driven at night, and he'd never really known why. Was it connected?

'Yeah, why is that?' he asked, trying to sound casual although his heart was starting to thud.

'Oh, the glare. If anything comes towards me, I just can't see—especially on wet roads. You know what it's like.'

'Well, we're all like that,' he said, feeling relieved for a moment until his father chipped in.

"Speak for yourselves,' he said. 'I'm all right. It can be tricky sometimes, of course, but I'm not like your mother. She really can't seem to see at night.' And then he tilted his head on one side. 'Are you having the same problem?'

Damn. Try to sound casual.

'Yeah, I might be. I went to the optician the other day for a routine check-up and mentioned that my night vision's been a bit off recently because I've been working so much in artificial light, and she asked if there was any family history, but I couldn't think of anything. I'd forgotten about your driving, Mum. It just didn't occur to me. Do you know if anyone else had anything like that?'

His mother shook her head. 'No, not that I can think of. Mike?'

'No. Nobody on my side.'

He felt a wave of relief. 'Oh, well, that's good. It doesn't sound like it if neither of you can think of anyone, so it's probably just coincidence. I expect I need to eat more carrots or something.'

'Oh, no, wait,' his mother said suddenly, and his heart sank. 'Your Great-Uncle George, perhaps, my mother's brother.'

'Did he have trouble with his eyes?'

'Not as far as I knew, and I know he used to read an awful lot, but he died in a freak car accident in his thirties. I seem to remember he'd been driving along a twisty country lane on a very sunny day and crashed into a tree on the edge of a wood. The person following behind said it was as if he hadn't seen the junction. It was in deep shade from the trees, but my mother always thought it might have been deliberate. I'll ask her about his sight, though. She might know more than me. So how bad is your night vision?' she added, getting to the nub of it in that way she had.

'Oh, it's not that bad,' he lied, feeling a little sick because he really, really hadn't wanted to hear any of that. 'It's probably just too much screen time. Everything we do now involves screens. My eyes are probably just tired.'

Or else it was the X-linked hereditary form of RP, which scarcely affected the female carrier but was passed down in spades to her sons. Damn.

'Hmm. Well, get it checked out properly if it doesn't get better, and I'll ask your grandparents. There certainly isn't anyone else I've ever heard of.'

He shrugged, trying to make light of it, not wanting to worry them. 'Don't worry about it. I've probably just got rubbish night vision like you, Mum, and Uncle George's accident was probably exactly that, or else Grandma's right and it was deliberate. Anyway, I'd better get back. I've got lots of stuff to do at home, and I'm on duty at six tomorrow,' he said, and made his escape.

Not that he had anything pressing to do at home, but he really didn't want to push his luck and drive at night in the lashing rain, because he hadn't been lying about that.

He got home as the light was fading, to find his porch light had come on. Laura's initiative purchase, which was working like a charm.

Hell, he'd missed her. He wanted nothing more than to go round to hers, but he wasn't going to, not after what he'd just found out. He went in, shut the door and opened his laptop. Time to do some research into X-linked sight loss...

He stuck it out until Monday evening, and then he cracked and called her.

'Hi. I didn't see you at work today. Are you OK?'

'Yes, of course I'm OK,' she said lightly. 'I just had a day off. How was your weekend?'

Not helpful, because he'd discovered things

he would rather not have known and researching further into it just made it worse. 'It was
fine,' he lied. 'Are you busy?'

There was a tiny hesitation, then she said,
'No, not really. Why?'

'I just wondered if you'd eaten.'

'No. I was about to, I've made a casserole,
but there's plenty. Want to join me?'

He was desperate to join her. 'That would be
lovely,' he said, and drove round a few minutes later, armed with a bottle of wine and a
fistful of excuses.

He didn't need them, because she didn't ask
any awkward questions. Didn't ask anything
at all, really, just smiled up at him and hugged
him when he walked through the door.

He wrapped her in his arms and held her
close, and she squeezed him tight.

'I've missed you,' she said softly. 'Are you
OK?'

'I'm fine,' he lied. 'I'm sorry, I was busy last
night. I've been neglecting things.'

Things like the fact that he hadn't got his
eyes checked out when he'd first started no-
ticing his night vision had deteriorated,
because he'd assumed it was tiredness, eye-

strain, working under artificial light, lack of beta-carotene—anything other than the truth. Hours of online research had reinforced that, and now to put the cherry on the cake there was the late Great-Uncle George, and a mother with slightly dodgy night vision who could be a barely symptomatic carrier of the faulty X-linked gene...

'Well, it's nice to have you back,' she murmured, and kissed him gently, her mouth soft and inviting under his, and her tenderness unravelled him.

They ended up in bed, the food forgotten. He lost himself completely in the comfort of her arms, buried himself in the warmth of her body, her passion and gentleness undoing him as he cradled her against his heart and hung on for dear life while wave after wave of sensation crashed over him, leaving him boneless and drained.

And then he realised he'd broken his golden rule, and fear swamped him. What if he'd made her pregnant? If he had RP, and he was increasingly convinced that he did, there was a fifty-fifty chance of him passing it on, and there was no way he'd wish this on anyone, least of all his own child.

'Laura, I'm useless. We didn't use anything, I just forgot—'

'Hey, it's OK. I'm on the Pill now,' she murmured reassuringly.

He studied her face, his panic receding a little. 'Are you sure?'

She laughed softly and leant over and kissed him, and he could taste her smile.

'Yes, Tom, I'm absolutely sure. I take it every day without fail.'

'I didn't mean that. I meant, are you absolutely sure it's all right? How long have you been on it?

'Oh—just over two weeks? So we should be OK.'

'Good, because I don't want to take any chances.'

'That's why I'm taking it, so we don't,' she said with another smile, and he heaved a sigh of relief, pulled her back into his arms and stopped worrying.

'Supper?' she said after a moment, and he nodded.

'That would be amazing. I've had another

hellish busy day. I think I need IV lunch. I never seem to get time to stop.'

'Well, you've got time now. I'll go and dish up while you get dressed.'

Laura walked into the kitchen, wrapped in her dressing gown and the rosy afterglow from their lovemaking.

He was back, and it was such a relief to know she'd been wrong.

There was nothing the matter, he clearly wasn't bored by her, and maybe he'd been genuinely busy. Whatever, she was more than happy to have him back, and she wasn't going to over-analyse it.

She dished up the casserole—made in the hope that he'd come round, but which she could have frozen if he hadn't—and sliced some of the fresh tiger bread she'd bought just in case.

She slathered it in butter, put it on the side of the bowls and put them on the table as he walked in, looking rumpled and sexy and good enough to eat.

He smiled at her. 'That smells amazing.'

'We aim to please.' She sat down at right angles to him and picked up her fork. 'So, tell me about your weekend. How were your parents?'

'Oh, they're fine. They're coming down in a couple of weeks to see my new place, and I told Mum about your grandfather's books and she'd love to see them, if that's OK?'

'Well—yes, of course it's OK,' she said, feeling a little shiver of something that felt like hope. If he was telling his parents about her, maybe...

And maybe not. Don't get carried away.

'Oh—you brought wine, didn't you? Would you like some?'

'That would be lovely, but just a small glass. I'm on at six tomorrow.'

'Me, too,' she said, with a flicker of relief that they seemed to be OK, because if not that would have made working together really, really awkward. She poured two small glasses and handed him one.

'Here you go. Don't drink it all at once.'

They chuckled, and he scooped up the last of his gravy with the bread.

'More?'

'Did you really need to ask?' he said, sliding his plate towards her, and she laughed because he looked as hopeful as Millie if there was a treat in the offing.

'No. Apparently not. More bread, too?'

'Oh, yeah. I'm starving.'

So she gave him most of the rest, had the last little scrapings herself with another slice of bread, and when they were done they curled up on the sofa, Millie between them with her head on his lap, and watched the tail-end of an old sitcom episode that had them both chuckling.

And it felt so good, so normal, almost like they were back in college living in the house-share, but with the added bonus of the after-glow of their lovemaking.

His hand was lying on Millie's back, stroking her gently on autopilot, and Laura reached out and threaded her fingers through his and he looked up and met her eyes.

She could see warmth and tenderness, and something else that she couldn't really read, but it sent a sudden shiver down her spine, a tiny tingle of unease.

Maybe she was wrong. Maybe it wasn't all OK, after all?

And then he sighed, and she could feel him

withdrawing from her. 'I need to go,' he said softly. 'Early start.'

She nearly asked him to stay, but there was that tingle of unease. 'It's OK. I'm on early, too.'

She followed him to the door, and he folded her against his chest and held her wordlessly for an age before he let her go.

'Sleep tight,' he murmured, and with a gentle, lingering kiss he opened the door and went out.

She watched his car pull away, the lights disappearing as he turned out of her drive, and then closed the door thoughtfully.

What was wrong? Something, she was sure, but he obviously wasn't about to discuss it. Had he found something out over the weekend? Maybe there was an eye problem with one of his relations that he hadn't known about—or maybe she was reading something into nothing.

She went back into the kitchen, cleared the table and loaded the dishwasher, took Millie out to the garden and then went back to bed, surrounded by the scent of his skin and the faint, lingering warmth of his body. Their lovemaking had been so emotionally charged tonight, as if there was a whole new element to it, something different that hadn't been there before.

Almost—desperation?

What's wrong, Tom? What's going on? What aren't you telling me?

CHAPTER SEVEN

BY THE MIDDLE of their shift the next day, she'd decided she'd imagined it.

He was fine, working with him was fine, and he was back to being his normal self. She must have read more into it than was there.

They were together in Resus, just finishing off the notes of the last case and speculating if they'd get time for lunch today, when the Tannoy burst into life.

'Adult trauma call, five minutes.'

'Here we go again. So much for lunch,' she said, her heart sinking, and went out to get the details.

She went back to Tom and the team who were assembling. 'Right, we've got a twenty-year-old man who lost control of his motorbike going down the steep hill to the prom, slid across the road, through the railings and ended up wedged on the sea defences. He has serious fractures of both legs and an arm, a flail chest and query pelvic fractures. We're going to need a radiographer here now, and if he makes it that far he'll need a full body CT scan and maybe MRI. We'll also need to activate massive transfusion protocol. Right, lead aprons everybody, because we're not going to be able to leave him for a second.'

Tom nodded. 'Is he conscious?'

'Not as far as I know, which could be a good thing for him if they've had to lift him off the rocks. Orthopaedics, Cardiothoracics and Neuro have been paged, they should be here any second. Are you OK to lead? It sounds pretty complex.'

'Yeah, sure. I've done a lot of stuff from HEMS while I was in London, it sounds pretty similar.'

By the time they'd finished donning their PPE and lead aprons and gearing up for all possibilities, their patient was being wheeled in, still with his helmet on.

'Has he been conscious at all?' Tom asked the paramedic after his handover, and he shook his head.

'No. His GCS has been three throughout.

The police are trying to contact his family. His name's Rob Wilding.'

'OK, thanks. Right, we'll need a full set of pictures of his head, spine, chest and pelvis, but let's get these clothes off first and find out what we're dealing with. Can I have the FAST scanner, please,' Tom was saying in the background, and she was glad he was there because she didn't fancy leading on the case and he'd had much more experience of this sort of thing than she had. The young man had so many issues that needed dealing with as a matter of urgency, and prioritising them was going to be tricky.

Both legs were splinted, the left fractured in multiple places, his right arm was lying at a very odd angle in a splint, and his breathing was laboured. That was possibly the most critical. That or a pelvic fracture with massive internal bleeding. Or a ruptured spleen...

'Oxygen sats eighty-eight per cent,' a nurse said, and Tom shook his head as the clothes were swiftly cut away to reveal a deep spreading bruise over his ribs. 'OK, he's got a large flail segment here. We need the CT team down here stat and we need to stabilise that flail segment, but we might need to intubate him and take over because he's not shifting nearly enough air so we need to know if we can get that helmet off yet. How's his trachea?'

'Displaced to the left,' Laura said, and Tom swore softly.

'So he's got a flail chest on the left and probably a pneumothorax on the right. Can I see those cranial and c-spine images, please?'

He looked across as the images that had just been taken appeared on the screen, and grunted.

'OK. His skull's cracked like an eggshell, but the occiput looks clear so it should be reasonably stable, and his neck looks good to go. Right, we need to get that helmet off. Laura, can you undo the strap and slide your hands in and stabilise his head and neck, please, while I take it off? Then he needs hundred per cent oxygen to get those sats up. OK, Rob, we're going to take your helmet off.'

It only took moments, but she was glad that Tom had the job of tilting it to clear his nose, and then it was away and they went back to what they were doing, and Tom was tutting.

'He's going to need a full body scan if we

can get him stable enough. Laura, can you put a chest drain in on that side, please? I just need to check his abdomen for free fluid, then I'll have a look at this arm next.'

'I'm already on it. That hand's not a good colour, is it?' she added as an aside as she started on the chest drain.

'No.' He picked up the arm carefully, felt for a pulse and shook his head. 'Nothing.' He checked the X-ray and winced. 'I'll see if I can pull it out quickly otherwise it'll have to wait and he might lose it.'

With a bit of gentle traction he managed to line up the arm again, to Laura's relief, and he nodded.

'OK, I've got a pulse,' he said, and while they put a cast on it to stabilise it he ran the FAST scanner over his abdomen. 'That looks OK at the moment. Now the legs. OK, they both have a pedal pulse but that's as good as it gets. Have you got that chest drain in, Laura?'

'In and bubbling nicely.'

'Any blood?'

'No, and his sats are picking up.'

'Well, there's a miracle, we don't have to intubate. Where the hell is everyone? We need Cardiothoracics and Orthopaedics in here now.'

And then suddenly the room was full of people, and after a combined effort of over an hour from when he'd been brought in, he was stable enough to take for a scan and then Theatre, where a multi-disciplinary team would work on him simultaneously.

Tom stepped back and watched as they wheeled him out, then turned and thanked everyone.

'Good job, everybody. Great teamwork. Well done. We've given him a chance, although who knows what's ahead of him,' he added, shaking his head. 'Right, I need lunch before I do anything else,' he muttered, and he stripped off his PPE and walked out, leaving her to finish off writing up the notes.

She stared after him, worried yet again. He'd been fine while they were busy, but now he seemed odd. Why? Because the boy might die? Or might live, but with life changing injuries?

'Is Tom OK?' Ryan asked, walking in a second later and looking concerned, and Laura shrugged.

'I don't know. He said he's gone to get some

lunch. We just saved a twenty-year-old by the skin of his teeth, but it's not looking good for him.'

'No, I noticed. What about you? Have you had lunch?'

'No. We were about to go when the trauma call came in.'

'Go now. Your hands are shaking.'

'I can't. I've got to finish this and then talk to the relatives.'

'No. Grab some chocolate or something and check on Tom, then come back and carry on if you must, but go now.'

She nodded and went to find him.

How was he still alive?

And why? Surely, *surely* he couldn't survive all those injuries and come out the other side the same person. The skull fracture alone was enough to kill him, without the major blood loss from the multiple limb fractures and the flail chest threatening to puncture the lung that still seemed to be working.

How was his pelvis intact? How were his internal organs still in one piece? How? Or had they just missed something massive brewing in the wings?

His whole body felt drained, and his hands were shaking, but at least the lad was in the right hands now. He just hoped they weren't saving him for a worse fate, because the chance of him not having life-changing injuries was pretty damn slim.

He went out to the snack dispenser in the waiting area and got a bar of chocolate, just as Laura appeared.

'Great minds think alike,' she said, and he ripped it open and passed her half, crammed the rest in his mouth then went back to the machine and bought another one and shared that, too, his hands shaking. Low blood sugar, or stress? Or both...

'Did you talk to the relatives?'

She shook her head. 'They aren't here yet. I don't know if the police have managed to track them down, but I just heard Rob made it to Theatre, and he's still stable.'

'How? *How?*'

She shrugged. 'I have no idea, Tom, and who knows what the future holds for him, but at least he might have one now. Ryan sent me to find you, by the way.'

'Ryan? Why? What did he want?'

'Just to check you were OK. He was worried about you.'

He frowned. 'Of course I'm OK. It's my job, it's what I do. I was just hungry. Right, do you want me to talk to the relatives when they turn up?'

'We could do it together?'

'OK. Not that there's much we can tell them at this stage apart from the fact that he's alive at the moment but probably has life-changing injuries. I hate giving that kind of news.'

'Don't we all? But it happens,' she said gently, her voice loaded with meaning. 'Things happen to people, Tom, and their lives change as a result, sometimes drastically, but life goes on and they learn to adapt.'

Do they? Would he? Would he learn to adapt to being blind?

Don't go there! It may not happen. You could be wrong. Or not...

'Actually, can you do it?' he asked, suddenly desperate to get away. 'I really need to get something proper to eat.'

'Only if you bring me back a sandwich.'

'Done.'

He threw her a smile and walked briskly away, heading out of the staff door into the park and sucking in the fresh air.

What if he was right? What if it *was* RP? And how long did he have before his life was changed for ever?

Don't think about it.

He didn't go round that evening, but he phoned her at nine to tell her that Rob Wilding had survived surgery to his left leg and chest wall, his head injury was stable and he was being moved to ICU.

And she cried.

'Laura?'

He heard a sniff. 'Sorry. I just can't believe he's alive. It doesn't seem credible.'

'No, tell me about it. He was really lucky it didn't kill him.'

'He was. His family will be so relieved now. They were utterly devastated. He's only had the bike three weeks, it was a birthday present.' She was silent for a moment, then he heard her take a deep breath. 'I don't suppose you want to come round?'

Want to? Yes. Was it wise? Probably not. 'It's late,' he said, stalling.

'I know, but—I could do with a hug. You could stay?' she added, and he felt an overwhelming surge of longing to spend the night in her arms.

Not wise, but so damn tempting.

He hesitated for an age, then he sighed quietly and gave up fighting it. 'OK. I'll come now. I'll see you in a minute.'

He grabbed his toothbrush and razor and deodorant, threw them in a washbag and stared at it for a second.

Thin end of the wedge...

To hell with it. He wanted her, she needed a hug and, dammit, so did he. He was going.

Not only did Rob survive, but forty-eight hours later, when they brought him very carefully out of the induced coma he'd been put into protect his brain, he was lucid and coherent.

He also had sensation and movement in both feet, and his hand which could so easily have lost viability also had feeling in it. Which, Tom thought, was nothing short of a miracle. And he didn't believe in them.

His parents came down to the ED to report on his progress, and by chance both he and Laura were on duty, so they were able to thank them personally for what they'd done.

'He was very lucky. We just did our job,' he said quietly, but his father shook his head.

'That's not how we see it. If you hadn't done what you did when you did and how you did it, he wouldn't have got to Theatre. That's what they told us. That's good enough for me. As far as we're concerned, you two saved our son's life—'

His voice cracked, and Tom wrapped his arms round him and gave him a brief, hard hug.

'That's what we're here for,' he said. 'It doesn't always work, but when it does, it makes it all worthwhile, so thank you for letting us know. It makes a real difference to us because we see so many people and have no idea what happens to them, so a success story like this is a real bonus. Give him our best wishes and tell him to come and see us when he's better.'

'We will,' his mother said, 'when he can

walk in here for himself, but that might be a while.' Her voice cracked, and she slipped her hand into her husband's. 'I tell you one thing. What's left of that bike is going to a scrap yard, and he's never having another one, not while I'm breathing. I don't ever want to have to see him like that again.'

'No. Nor do we,' Laura said with a wry smile, and she hugged his mother gently. 'You take care.'

'We will. And thank you, again.'

They walked away hand in hand, and Tom watched them go with a lump in his throat. 'It must be so tough being a parent.'

'Absolutely. Well, if you're a proper parent,' she added with an edge to her voice. 'It's not tough being my mother. She's never had a clue what's going on in my life, and she wouldn't care if she did. Right, what's next?'

If they hadn't been at work he would have hugged her, but he had the distinct feeling that if he did she'd just cry, and he didn't want to do that to her. Plus the gossips would have a field day, and so far, as far as he was aware, they didn't know they were anything other than old friends, and that was the way he wanted it to

stay, at least until after he'd had his referral appointment, because that could change things
drastically.

So he didn't hug her, not then, but that evening he took her down to the sea front and they
ate fish and chips on a bench overlooking the
sea, with Millie at their feet looking hopeful,
and after they'd eaten they stayed there for a
while, and he laid his arm along the back of
the bench behind her, not touching her but just
there, so that his thumb could stroke the top of
her arm without being wildly obvious.

'Do you have any idea how sexy that is?' she
murmured, and he chuckled.

'Apparently not. Time to go home?'

And then he stopped in his tracks.

Home? Where had that come from?

It was all getting way too cosy, too comfortable, too looking like they had a future, and
then when he got his diagnosis and it all blew
up in his face, what then?

He removed his arm and straightened up.
'Or maybe we should both get an early night,'
he added, and she turned to look at him and
searched his eyes.

'If that's what you want,' she said quietly, and he nodded.

'It's been a hectic week. I'm bushed. Maybe tomorrow.'

He'd said home.

And then he'd changed. It was like flicking a switch, and she felt sick.

What's going on?

Because something was. Something must be, to make him change like that. She didn't think it was to do with his eyes this time, either. Was it because of Karen and the way she'd treated him? Was he just wary because he'd stayed the night again and brought a washbag? Maybe, and that wouldn't be a surprise. She was wary, too, after Pete, but maybe not wary enough. Maybe she should be less accommodating, less eager. Less available.

So the following day she invented a reason why she couldn't see him that evening, and spent the whole of it wallowing in self-pity and calling herself a fool. She could have been with him, strengthening the bond between them, giving him the confidence to trust her. Instead she'd held him at arm's length and pushed him away, and now she had a run of night duty coming up and she'd missed her chance.

Idiot.

He got his referral appointment, but it wasn't for another three weeks and he wasn't sure he could stand the suspense that long, so he rang them, explained that he worked at the hospital and could take a cancellation at minimal notice, and sat back to wait.

Which just made the suspense worse—on top of which Laura was being a bit funny with him.

Not distant, exactly, but maybe less—welcoming?

No. Wrong word. Less spontaneous. More guarded.

Maybe that was a good thing, because when—no, if—they told him he had RP, he'd need to cool things between them substantially, because he knew perfectly well that she'd brush her own needs aside and stick by him, and he couldn't do that to her. Not so early in their relationship, and maybe never.

He didn't want to be a burden on her. On anyone.

Don't jump the gun. You don't even know yet.

Except he did, in his heart of hearts, because he'd seen the images and done a ton of research, and he knew what he'd seen. And there was Great-Uncle George. What he didn't know was how long it would take to lose his sight, and nobody could tell him that. He was going to have to find out the hard way.

Their shift patterns didn't coincide for the next week because she was on nights and so he hardly saw her. They spoke on the phone and he'd been round to hers a couple of times, but he'd been plagued by his conscience and he'd deliberately avoided being in a situation where it would be natural for them to make love.

He just couldn't do it, not while he was sitting on this. He hadn't told her about George because he didn't want to worry her, so it almost felt like he was living a lie, but what else could he do? Nothing, until he knew, and there was no sign of a cancellation appointment, so he stalled and avoided her, and then just after two on Friday afternoon, he had a call from the clinic to say they'd had a late cancellation, come now.

He told James he was leaving early without telling him why, walked out of the department and into a barrage of tests and investigations, and then they sat him down and took away any last hope he had that he'd been wrong.

He had retinitis pigmentosa, and there was every probability, given the history of his great-uncle George and his mother, that it was the hereditary X-linked type.

And just like that all his hopes and dreams for his career, for a family, for a future with Laura, crumbled into dust. He was going to go blind, and there was nothing anyone could do about it.

He walked home in a daze, arriving at the same time as his food order. He'd forgotten about it, forgotten that his parents were coming this weekend, forgotten everything.

He put the food away on autopilot, his mind numb. He'd already blitzed the house, but he cleaned it again for something to do, shifted his things into the spare bedroom and remade the bed for his parents, and then finally he rang Laura.

She'd finished her shift and now had a long weekend, so he phoned to check it was still

OK for them to go round on Saturday after lunch for his mother to look at the books. Not that he really needed to remind her, but he just wanted to hear her voice.

'I just wanted to remind you my parents are up this weekend. Is it still OK for us to come round?' he asked her.

'It's fine. I was expecting you all. It'll be lovely showing the books to someone who'll appreciate them, and she may be able to tell me a bit more about some of them.'

'Are you sure?'

'Absolutely. I'm looking forward to it. Just come whenever. I'll be in.'

He wanted to go now. He was desperate to tell her, to get it over with, but it wouldn't be fair, not with his parents coming. He'd do it after they left. Sit her down and tell her they had no future. But not now...

'That'll be great. Thanks. She's really looking forward to it, too,' he said, and hung up quickly before his voice cracked and betrayed him.

She made a lemon drizzle cake for them. It had always been her grandfather's favourite, and since they were coming to look at his books it felt appropriate, if a little unsettling.

The last time she'd made one was for his funeral, and she ended up drizzling a little herself as she poured the syrup over it. Stupid, really. He was better off now, and she was just being sentimental and maudlin.

She put it on the windowsill out of Millie's reach for the syrup to soak in, then went into the study, armed with a duster and the cobweb brush. Goodness knows how long it was since she'd even looked in there, far less sat in there talking to him as she had so many times since he'd died.

Because of Tom? Had his presence filled the yawning void in her life, or had she moved on? Maybe a bit of both, she acknowledged as she dusted, because the books just brought back fond memories now, not waves of aching loneliness.

Progress, she told herself, and once it was all clean and tidy she went and showered, had a bite of lunch and then went back in the study to look at the books again.

There were some she hardly remembered, some in boxes on the top shelves where they were most protected from the light, and they were the ones she was most curious about. Maybe she'd get Tom's mother to look at those first.

The doorbell rang and she went and opened the door, and beside Tom was an older version of him and a tiny, delicate woman with the same beautiful slate blue eyes.

'You must be Laura,' she said, smiling at her with Tom's smile as she shook her hand. 'I'm Katherine, and this is Mike.'

'Hi. It's lovely to meet you both. Come on in.'

They stepped inside, and then Katherine looked past Laura, took a step forward and then hesitated. 'May I?'

Laura laughed. 'Of course. That's why you're here. Let's go and have a look. Tom, I don't suppose you could make tea?'

He nodded and the men left them to it, and his mother didn't speak again for several minutes, just looked along all the shelves, shaking her head from time to time and smiling.

'What an amazing, eclectic collection. He must have been a fascinating man.'

'He was,' she said, welling up a little. 'He

knew all of the books, and I must have spent hours with him as a child poring over them.'

'He let you look at them?'

'Oh, yes. Well, lots of them. Not the ones in boxes, although he showed them to me once or twice, when I was older—maybe fifteen? There's a Shakespeare one, if I remember rightly.'

Katherine looked at her keenly. 'Would you mind showing it to me?'

'No, of course not. It's up here,' she said, dragging a chair over to the shelves and climbing on it. 'I think this is the one.'

She lifted down the heavy leather box and Katherine took it from her, laid it on the desk on top of a cloth she'd spread out there, and put on her gloves. Then she carefully opened the box, lifted out the old leather-bound book, placed it on the cloth and opened it.

And gasped softly.

'Laura!' she said, her voice hushed. 'Do you have any idea what this is?'

'Well—Shakespeare's plays, I know that much, but no, not really. No more than that. He said it was rare.'

She bent over it beside Katherine, and noticed that her fingers were trembling slightly as they traced the name of the publisher.

Herringman. It meant nothing to her, but it meant something very significant to Katherine. She turned a few pages, then straightened up and met Laura's eyes.

'My dear girl, do you have any idea what this book is worth?'

She shook her head. 'No, not really. A few thousand, maybe? I don't know.'

'Much more than that. Given the right auction house, this book would fetch somewhere in the region of a hundred and fifty to two hundred thousand, maybe more.'

She stared at her in astonishment. 'What? How—why?'

Katherine laughed softly. 'Because it's a priceless first edition folio and it would be hugely sought after.'

Good grief. She sat down on the chair before her legs gave way. 'I don't believe it. I had no idea it was worth that much. He's had it ages. I think his father bought it—and there are others, too, but this was his favourite and probably most precious.'

'Does that mean you want to keep it? Because if so, it really, really ought to be stored in a controlled atmosphere.'

'I—I...'

She looked up, dazed, and Tom was propped against the doorframe with a strange smile on his face.

'I told you, you should have them valued,' he murmured, and her eyes welled.

'He said he was leaving them to me, and he made me promise that I'd look after them, and if I ever wanted to sell them, I'd have to be very careful who I sold them to. I can understand why now, but... Wow. So much money? That's ridiculous.'

Tom chuckled softly and shook his head.

'What've you done to her, Mum? I think she needs a cup of tea. I'll put the kettle on again.'

She stared at the book, then back at Tom.

'I think that would be a good idea. I can't... That's... I'm speechless.'

She heard Tom laugh again as he walked away. 'That'll be the day,' he said, not unkindly, and she got up and followed him into the kitchen.

'I don't believe it,' she said, and he took one

look at her, wrapped his arms around her and pressed a kiss to her head.

'You don't have to sell them.'

She rested her head on his shoulder and sighed. 'But—I can't keep them. Not the ones like that. They're too important, and I know nothing about them, they don't mean anything to me. It would be wrong to keep them. They're wasted on me.'

'Then sell them, but you don't have to do anything in a hurry, you know that. And you can trust my mother. She knows her stuff.'

She nodded, still stunned. 'He was going to catalogue them, but he never got round to it and then he ran out of time because he couldn't see…'

She felt his arms tighten a little in support, and blinked away tears she had no intention of shedding. 'I had absolutely no idea they were worth anything like that amount. A few hundred, maybe some of them a few thousand— it's crazy. And what about insurance?'

'You will have to consider insurance,' Katherine said from behind her, and she eased out of Tom's arms and turned to his mother.

'I will, won't I?' She rolled her eyes. 'He's up

there laughing at me, I can hear him,' she said, and reached for the kettle. 'Tea, everyone?'

His mother spent the rest of the afternoon going through the books, and came back alone on Sunday morning, leaving the men tackling the garden at Tom's cottage, and by lunchtime she'd compiled a list of books which were of particular value. The Shakespeare one was the jewel in the crown, but there were other minor gems, too, with much more modest estimates.

'I know someone who could be interested in the Shakespeare book, if you ever decide to sell it,' Katherine told her. 'May I mention it to him?'

'Um—I'm not sure. I don't really know what to do.'

'You don't have to do anything, but it might be interesting to know what he'd be prepared to pay for it.'

It would. 'OK, but just make sure he knows I haven't decided.'

Katherine smiled. 'I will. And don't worry. It's in good condition, and the climate in the room is obviously fairly well suited to it, so it's not coming to any harm where it is, but you do need to consider insurance. I'll send you a valuation. And now I think I'm going to have to stop, or Mike'll go home without me.'

'Oh, no, you must. I'm so sorry. I didn't mean to take your entire weekend. I feel really guilty.'

'Don't feel guilty! I've had a wonderful time. And remember what I said. Here. You can ring me whenever.'

She put a business card on the desk, and Laura tucked it inside her address book.

'Thank you. I will. And I can't thank you enough for what you've done this weekend. I'm still stunned.'

'Laura, you're welcome. And if you want any more advice, if you change your mind about anything, then ring me. I'll always be happy to help you.'

'Thank you.'

She gave Katherine a hug, waved her off and then closed the door, the dog at her side.

'What do you think of that, Millie?'

Millie wagged her tail and whined, and she stroked the soft, gentle head. 'You need a walk, don't you? And so do I. My head's a mess. And I might just set the burglar alarm.'

* * *

'How did you get on?'

'Oh, really well. She's a lovely girl, Tom, and you could do a great deal worse. Well, you did. That Karen creature. But Laura—she's perfect for you.'

He looked away, busying himself with the kettle, fighting with the lump in his throat because there was no hope for him and Laura now. 'It's not like that. We're just friends, colleagues.'

'Rubbish. She adores you. And I saw how you looked at her.'

'I'm very fond of her—always have been. I've known her since uni. We're just friends, you know that.'

'Well, give yourselves time.'

'Mum, it's not going anywhere,' he said firmly.

His mother made one of those noises, a little humph that told him quite clearly what she really thought, and he poured boiling water into the cups, stirred the teabags and lifted them out without a comment.

'Right, you take the tea, I'll bring the sandwiches,' he said, and they went out into the garden.

'Oh, this looks better.'

'It should do, we've been working on it all morning. Dad's in the shower, he'll be down in a minute. We found a bench under that tree. Let's go and sit on it and wait for him, it should be dry enough. Ah, here he is at last,' he said with relief, only too ready to change the subject. 'Dad, I've got a cup of tea here for you and some sandwiches. Come and join us.'

His father sat down and ate his sandwiches, picked up the mug and eyed him thoughtfully over the top of it.

'What's going on, Thomas?' he asked after an age. 'You've been acting strangely all weekend.'

Tom swallowed and looked away. 'No, I haven't.'

'Rubbish. What is it? Is it the eye thing?'

'Mike—shh!' his mother hissed, but Tom gave up, put his tea down on the grass and let out a slightly ragged sigh.

'Yes,' he said gently, 'it's the eye thing. I saw the specialist on Friday, and it turns out I've got retinitis pigmentosa. It's a progressive deterioration of the rods and cones in the retina, and it starts with night blindness and poor peripheral vision, and then shrinks in until eventually you can be left with just minimal central vision or none at all.'

'So what can they do?' his father asked, ever practical.

He glanced up at him and then looked away again. 'Nothing. Absolutely nothing. My eyes will deteriorate gradually and over the next decade or so I'm going to lose most of my sight, and there's nothing anyone can do about it.'

'Oh, Tom, no...' His mother's mug slipped out of her fingers and fell onto the grass, splashing him, and he heard a strangled sob. 'It's my fault, isn't it?' she asked, her voice cracking, and he didn't know what to say. Nothing that would help.

'No. No, it's not your fault, Mum. You weren't to know.'

She sat back, turned to face him and stared straight into his eyes, her own awash with grief. 'It is inherited?' she asked bluntly, and he gave a resigned sigh and nodded.

'Yes. Yes, it looks as if it's inherited. They think that's probably what caused your uncle to crash. Going from bright light to dark is a classic. It's likely he just didn't see the bend.'

'So—will your children inherit it?' she asked tentatively, and he shook his head.

'No. No, they won't, because I won't have any, which is why it's going nowhere with Laura—'

His voice broke and he looked away, unable to hold her eyes, unable to hold anything, most particularly a conversation about this. He dumped his tea on the grass, walked inside and upstairs to his bedroom, lay down on the bed and stared blindly at the ceiling.

Laura. His dear, darling, beautiful Laura. Ever faithful, ever loyal, never shirking her duty to anyone. He'd have to tell her, but how? His mother and father were broken-hearted, it would break her heart, too, and like them she'd want to stand by him—and he couldn't let her. Couldn't. It wasn't fair.

So he'd have to tell her, somehow. She had to know, and she had to know now, so she had time to get her act together before she was back at work at lunchtime tomorrow.

There was a knock on the door, and his father came in, his face creased with worry.

'Are you all right, Tom? Is there anything we can do?'

He shook his head and sat up. 'No. No, I'll be fine, Dad. I just need to get used to the idea. It'll progress slowly, I'll have time to acclimatise, but for now I'm fine and it could take years. Decades. I might never go completely blind.'

Or it could be as little as five or ten years.

'Will you be able to work?'

'Yes. Yes, for years. It's very slow.' He hoped...

His father was nodding slowly, the information sinking in bit by bit. He frowned. 'Look, we need to go, we're out for dinner tonight and we can't get out of it, but your mother's very upset. You need to come and talk to her, Tom. Reassure her.'

Reassure her? He was struggling to reassure himself, never mind anyone else. And he still had to talk to Laura.

He got to his feet, squeezed his father's shoulder on the way past and ran downstairs to find his mother with her hands in the kitchen sink, sobbing silently into the washing up.

'Come here,' he said softly, and turned her

into his arms and hugged her as she cried for him. Then he mopped her up, sat her down with his father and told them everything he knew about what was going to happen to him. Well, most of it.

He saw them off an hour later, after another cup of tea and more tears, then had a shower and changed and walked round to Laura's. He didn't know if she'd be in, and if she wasn't he'd just sit and wait, but he didn't want to talk to her on the phone. She'd ask what was wrong, and he'd break down. Dammit, he'd probably do it anyway. He was hanging by a thread.

But she was in, and as she opened the door and saw him her smile faltered, and his heart broke.

He looked awful.

So awful that something dreadful must have happened, and he'd been weird all weekend. Falsely jolly, and yet when he'd hugged her once or twice he'd held her really tight.

'Are you busy? I just—wanted to see you.'

She beckoned him in wordlessly, closed the

door behind him and searched his eyes. 'Talk to me, Tom.'

He let his breath out on a shaky sigh and got straight to the point. 'They had a cancellation on Friday.'

'Oh, Tom…' She reached out her arms, but he took a step back.

'Don't—' His voice cracked and he turned away, walking through to the kitchen and standing staring out across the garden while her heart broke for him. She followed him.

'Tom, I—'

'Please don't say anything, Laura. I don't want your sympathy. I can't deal with it. I just wanted you to know.'

She walked quietly over to him, tuned him towards her and put her hands on his face.

'Look at me.'

He opened his eyes, and they were glistening with tears, the lashes clumped, his irises the colour of dark, rain-washed slate. His beautiful eyes, so expressive, so tender one minute, so filled with laughter the next, were drained of light. And he was terrified.

'Oh, Tom,' she said softly. She went up on

tiptoe and kissed his eyes, one by one, and then wrapped him in her arms and cried for him.

'Don't.'

'Why? Why can't I cry for you, my love?'

'I'm not your love—'

She tipped her head back and looked at him. 'Yes, you are. You know that. I love you, Tom. I've loved you since I first met you, and nothing's changed that. I just love you more now, now I know who you really are.'

'And who the hell am I, Laura?' he asked, pushing her away. 'A broken, washed-up, redundant, useless waste of space—'

'No! Stop it, Tom. Just stop right there and listen to me. You are not broken! You are not washed up, or redundant, or useless! How good is your sight now?'

He frowned. 'Now? Now, it's fine, but it isn't going to be, is it? My night vision isn't great already. You know that.'

'No. Well, that's OK, because we have technology now and the power of electricity at our fingertips, so your night vision isn't really an issue. And it could be years before your sight deteriorates to any significant extent. Decades. If you even lose your sight.'

'When, Laura. Not if, when. And I don't *want* you to love me. I can't give you anything. I have nothing to offer you. Nothing. I have no idea what the future holds for me, and there's no way I want you saddled with me out of pity—'

'I don't pity you! I'm sorry you've got this, desperately sorry, of course I am, but you can deal with this. You have the strength and determination to deal with it, and you'll be fine. And saddled with you? Dream on. Being with someone you love when they're going through something difficult is not *saddled*. It's a privilege. We can do this together.'

'You don't know what you're talking about—'

'Don't be ridiculous, of course I do. My grandfather was blind, remember? So I know *exactly* what I'm talking about. Being able to help him be independent and mobile and happy was a joy. He was never a burden, not for a single minute.'

He shook his head, his eyes raw with grief. 'You don't understand. That isn't it. My great-uncle was starting to go blind when he died in a car accident. He drove into the dense shade of trees on a sunny day, and he couldn't see the bend. There's a very high probability that he had it, and that my mother, who never drives at night because she can't see well enough, is a carrier. If it's hereditary, I can never have children. My mum will never be a grandmother, I'll never be a father—I can't do that to you. You need to be free, Laura. Free to find someone who can give you the family you deserve. I'm no good to you. I'm no good to anyone. You don't need me. I don't want you to need me.'

'Well, I do. I do need you, Tom. And anyway, you're making some sweeping assumptions. I've never said I want children. I'm not sure I do. I don't think I'd even know how to be a mother, so you can put that out of your mind. And anyway, before you condemn yourself to a solitary life, have you had any genetic tests?'

He shook his head, then shrugged. 'They took all sorts of bloods and stuff, but I won't get any results for a while and it may not show anyway, but I know, Laura. I know that's what he had, and his sister handed the gene down to my mother, but because they're both female they're just barely symptomatic carriers, but

I'm not, I'm going to go blind, and there's nothing anyone can do about it.'

'There may be, though, soon,' she said, refusing to give up on him. 'There's research going on, clinical trials of drugs, gene therapy, stem cell work—so much. There will be a cure, Tom. One day, there will be a cure.'

'But not now, and not in time, certainly not for me and maybe not for any children I had, and I can't let that happen. I can't have children and know they or their children could go blind. You don't know what it means.'

'Don't know what it means? Of course I know what it means, Tom! My grandfather was severely visually impaired. I know all about it, what you will and won't be able to do, and it will be fine! I promise you, it will be all right. We can make it all right. And maybe if you need one, down the line, you could get a guide dog like Millie to look after you and keep you safely independent.'

He looked down at Millie, sat leaning against his leg, and he reached down to her and stroked her head. 'Did you keep him safe, poppet? What a good girl.'

Her tail waved tentatively, and she licked his hand.

'She looks worried,' he said, his face creasing in concern.

'Yes, of course she's worried. You're upset and she knows that and she loves you, Tom. Come on, let's sit down and I'll make you a cup of tea and we can talk this through.'

He looked at her, and she could see longing in his eyes. Longing, and hesitation.

'I need to go home,' he said eventually, as if the words were dragged from him.

She shook her head. 'No. Stay with me. Let's forget the tea. Come to bed, let me hold you.'

'I can't.'

'Yes, you can. You need me, Tom, and I need you.'

He closed his eyes, and she took his hand and led him into the bedroom and lay down with him in her arms, and he gave a shuddering sigh and rested his head against hers.

'I've been wanting to tell you since Friday, but I couldn't, not with my parents here, and I've been so…'

'Alone?' she finished for him, and he nodded.

'Yes. And scared. I hate the dark, always

have, and the thought of it… I've missed you. I needed you so much.'

She felt her heart ache for him, and her hand reached up and cradled his jaw. 'Shh. It's all right. I've missed you, too, but I'm here for you, and I'll always be here.'

As long as he'd let her…

CHAPTER EIGHT

HE STAYED THAT NIGHT, but he left early on Monday morning and she didn't see him again until Tuesday, and they were too busy then to do more than catch up briefly. Yet again their shifts didn't line up, so the next day he was on late, she was on early, and she overslept and got there in the nick of time.

She was working with Livvy, and as usual it was hectic, but then they suddenly found themselves with some breathing space.

'Coffee while the going's good?' Livvy said, and she nodded, relieved to have time to stop and also that she had someone to talk to so she wasn't constantly dwelling on Tom.

'Absolutely. I'm starving, I overslept and there wasn't time for breakfast. I hate early mornings after I've had a run of nights.'

'Oh, me, too. Come on. James, we're taking a break,' she said, and they headed out of the door before he had time to reconsider.

They went through the hospital to the Park Café because it was windy, but the second they walked in Laura felt queasy. It smelt hot and greasy, and she grabbed a banana and a chocolate muffin, ordered a coffee and headed for the door to the park.

'Are you OK if we sit outside? I fancy some fresh air,' she said, and Livvy shrugged.

'OK. It's a bit draughty, but that's fine.'

It was draughty, but she hauled in the fresh air and felt instantly less weird. 'Oh, that's better. I don't know what's wrong with me, I feel jetlagged after my nights. Must be low blood sugar.'

She picked up her coffee, lifted it to her lips and pulled a face. She didn't fancy it at all, so she ate the banana, then ripped the muffin open and ate a bite.

'Better?' Livvy asked, sipping her fruit tea and picking the grapes out of her fruit pot.

'Much.' She picked the coffee up again, took a sip and pulled a face. 'Oh, that tastes revolting, I can't drink it,' she said and pushed it away, and Livvy's eyes widened.

'You're not pregnant, are you?'

Laura stared at her friend, startled, and shook her head. 'No—no, of course I'm not! How could I be pregnant?'

'Um—the usual way?'

'But—I couldn't...'

'Oh, come on,' Livvy said with a teasing smile, 'everybody knows you and Tom are an item. You can't keep anything like that secret in this place.'

'But—no, I can't be. It's not possible. There must be something funny with the water. It's been odd at home for a couple of days. It happens sometimes.'

Livvy looked unconvinced, but Laura's mind was whirling.

Could she be? No! How?

She had another sip of the coffee, got rid of the taste with a bite of muffin and then ate the rest to try and settle her roiling stomach. She'd get a drink from the water cooler when they got back to the ED. She was probably just thirsty.

Or pregnant...

Seriously?

* * *

Tom came on at twelve, but he was working with Sam and she was in cubicles, so she didn't see him to speak to, which was a relief. She had no idea what to say to him, and frankly saying nothing seemed like the best idea, at least until she knew if she was pregnant. And anyway, she felt OK now. It must have been low blood sugar.

The next day she was fine, so she heaved a sigh of relief, ate a nicely carb-laden breakfast and went to work, and found herself with Tom again.

'Hi, stranger. How are you?'

'Fine,' she said, relieved that it was the truth. 'You?'

'Oh, I'm OK. My shoulder's a bit stiff from all the gardening at the weekend. I think I pulled something, but it looks good. You ought to come round and see it. Fancy supper?'

'That would be lovely. Can I bring Millie?'

'Of course you can. I love her, you know that.'

'She loves you, too. She lies with her head on the back of the sofa watching people passing by, and I can always tell if it's you coming by the crazy waggy tail.'

He chuckled. 'So what do you fancy? I've got some salmon fillets, or we can get a takeaway?'

'Salmon would be lovely. I ought to go and get on, I'm in cubicles again with Livvy— unless you need me in Resus, in which case give me a shout.'

'OK, will do.'

She went back to the work station, and was immediately cornered by Livvy.

'Well?'

'Well what?'

'Are you?'

'No—shh! I'm fine,' she said under her breath. 'I told you I wasn't.'

'Hmm. Still unconvinced. Have you done a test?'

'No—and would you shut up? We can't talk about this here,' she whispered desperately, 'and anyway, there's nothing to talk about.'

Livvy hmphed, grinned at her and grabbed the next set of notes and walked away, still smiling, and Laura shook her head, finished up her notes on the computer and went back to check on a patient.

* * *

It was a glorious evening, and they ate outside at the rickety old table he'd found in the shed, pulled up against the equally ancient bench.

He'd baked the salmon in a parcel, and cooked some tiny new potatoes and fine green beans to go with it. Clean, wholesome and delicious, and she was more than ready for it because her blood sugar was teetering again.

She cleared her plate, then put her knife and fork down and pushed it away.

'That was delicious. Thank you.'

'Pudding?' he asked, and she had a moment of doubt.

'What is it?'

'Apple pie. I wasn't going to buy it, but it looked so good. And I've got ice cream in the freezer.'

'Sounds good. No ice cream,' she added, because she just didn't fancy the sound of it. 'Is the pie cold?'

'Yes, it's in the fridge.'

'Perfect. Cold apple pie and a cup of tea?'

'Coming right up,' he said, and took their plates away, Millie at his heels just on the off-chance that he might drop the odd scrap by accident.

'Don't give her anything,' she called after him, and she heard him talking to the dog. It sounded like he was apologising to her for being mean, and she chuckled.

They came back together, Millie looking super-attentive and Tom looking just the teeniest bit guilty. He put the tray down and passed her her plate without looking at her, and she bit her lip.

'Millie, stop begging,' he said, and she laughed at him.

'You are so naughty. What did you give her?'

'Nothing dreadful. There was a little potato that had fallen in the sink, that's all.'

'That's all it takes, isn't it, Millie? You're a piglet.'

'She's lovely and slender.'

'Because she doesn't get scraps all the time and has a balanced diet suitable for a dog of her size and age,' she said pointedly, but she was still laughing and he had the grace to join in.

'What time are you on tomorrow?' he asked as they finished eating.

'Eight till six. How about you?'

'Ditto. I've got a normal day shift for once.'

She tilted her head on one side. 'Want to stay at mine?'

He hesitated, then shook his head. 'No. I'll walk you home, though. I'll just put this lot in the dishwasher and we can go.'

He didn't stay the night.

It would have been too cosy, too domesticated, too—hell, too much like a real relationship, one with a future, and it just wasn't fair to do that to her.

It didn't stop him wanting to make love to her, though. Didn't stop him wanting to take her to bed and show her with his body how much he cared. Didn't stop him wanting her all the next day, just like he did every day.

But he couldn't have her, and he knew that, so he didn't stay, and he didn't make love to her. He was just glad they hadn't got together seven years ago when he'd had no idea. They could have had children by now, and the thought that he could have passed the gene on to them filled him with horror.

Not that he'd had any results, yet, but he'd been warned it would take a while, and anyway, he knew. His grandmother had remembered a few other things about Great-Uncle George, like his clumsiness and the way he'd never seemed to be able to see in the evening unless the lights were bright, and the time he'd stepped out in front of a car because he hadn't seen it out of the corner of his eye.

Nothing on its own to make you think, but enough together to build a convincing picture. And he was convinced.

Convinced, and heartbroken, because of Laura.

Laura, who loved him. Laura, who wanted to be with him to help him navigate what was to come. Laura, who said she didn't want children when she would have been a brilliant mother.

He couldn't let her sacrifice herself for him. It wasn't fair, and he needed to distance himself from her. Harder than it sounded, because she wasn't having any of it, and he was too weak to resist her.

Too weak, too needy to ignore her, but too much in love with her to want her hurt in any way, and she would be.

And the next day, of course, they were working together, so he wouldn't be able to ignore her, but he wouldn't see her afterwards. He'd make some excuse, try and put a little distance between them for her sake...

He didn't stay, so she got up early and took Millie for a run, then washed, dressed, made herself some tea and toast and forced herself to eat it, but the tea was weird again so she threw it down the sink and took a bottle of water with her to work. She obviously needed to run the water for longer, or rinse out the kettle. Maybe it needed descaling again.

But it happened again in her break, when she went to the café, and it happened again the next day, and the next, and she was beginning to wonder if Livvy had been right.

She wasn't working with Tom that day, thank goodness, but the possibility that she'd run into him was making her feel sick with dread, and every now and again she'd hear his voice and her chest would squeeze with pain. She couldn't be. He'd be devastated, and so would she. It couldn't be happening.

And then the next morning she was sick.

No. Please, no. She couldn't be. Could she?

She made herself eat something plain, went

to work and was supposed to be in Resus, but that worried her because she'd be exposed to X-rays all the time, so she couldn't just ignore it and hope it would go away.

She made it through the rest of the shift without having to make any excuses to leave the room, and escaped on time for a change, and after she'd got home and walked Millie she drove to the supermarket on the edge of town and bought some more fruit—and a pregnancy test.

Not that she could be, but...

She was.

There it was, on the wand, clear as day.

PREGNANT

How?

She had absolutely no idea. She'd taken her Pill without fail, at the same time every day, or within an hour or so.

Except the day young Rob Wilding had been brought in, the lad on the motorbike. But that was only a little more than three weeks ago. How could she be feeling queasy so soon? Unless she'd already been pregnant by then?

She walked out of the bathroom, sat down

on the edge of the bed and stared blankly at the wall. This couldn't be happening to her! There was no way she could be pregnant!

Except she was, apparently. Just like her mother.

She'd always vowed she'd never be like her mother, and yet there she was, alone, pregnant and without a proper permanent job, so no maternity leave, no job protection, no income apart from statutory maternity benefit which was barely enough to survive on—and Tom.

And knowing he was the father was no comfort, because she knew exactly how he'd react, and she was dreading it.

Numb, she got up and walked stiffly out of the bedroom to the study, and curled up in her grandfather's old chair, desperate for his sane and loving presence, his sound advice, his unconditional love for her.

'Oh, Grumps, what am I going to do?' she asked, but he couldn't help her.

Except he already had, she realised. She'd given up her permanent job and come up here to look after him until he'd died, but he was still looking after her as he always had. Still there for her, in the roof over her head and the means to feed herself and her child. She had a home of her own, and enough money tied up in his precious book collection to support her and her baby for years, if it came to that.

Maybe it wouldn't. Maybe Tom would change his mind about them when he knew, or at the very least support his child, but if not, she'd still be all right.

'Thank you, Grumps,' she whispered, and swiped away a tear. 'And don't worry about me. I'm not going to be like her. I won't, I promise. I'll be the best mother I can be, and I'll tell him or her all about you and how good you were to me.'

And she had to tell Tom.

She didn't want to, she didn't have a clue how to, but she had to tell him. Not today. It was too late today. She'd do it tomorrow. She wasn't at work then and neither was Tom. She'd ring him in the morning.

Laura.

Why was she ringing him? He was trying to avoid her, but it was hard to keep any distance. He saw her every day at work, but he'd spoken to James and asked him to alter their shifts so they didn't work together, and it was killing him.

Luckily James hadn't asked any questions apart from 'Are you OK?', which he'd slightly sidestepped, but she was still there, still in the department at the same time for at least part of most days, and he was on edge all day, torn between wanting to see her and dreading hearing her voice because it just made him want to cry with frustration.

It was excruciating. Gut-wrenching. And now she was phoning him on his day off, just to torture him even more.

Why? What did she want?

His phone went to voicemail, so he gave it a minute and listened to her message.

'Tom, hi. Um—I need to talk to you about something. Can you call me, please?'

That was it. Very calm, very level, very Laura.

He listened to it again, just to hear her voice, and detected an edge to it that he hadn't noticed before.

What did they need to talk about? There

was nothing to say, or at least nothing that he wanted to say to her he hadn't already said, because he knew she'd do what Laura always did, and turn into the Good Samaritan riding to the rescue without a thought for her own happiness.

She'd done it for friends at uni, she'd done it for her grandfather, and he was damned if he'd let her make the same sacrifice for him, because he'd be asking far more of her than they ever had.

He'd be asking her to give up any hope of them having a family of their own, and that was wrong, so wrong, because she'd be an amazing mother. He'd seen her with children, he knew how much she cared, how passionately she felt about the appalling way her mother had treated her and the way her grandfather had had to step in.

So what should he do? Call her? Ignore her? Go round, on the off-chance?

Yeah. Maybe that was it. Go round. That way he could read her body language, find out what she was really saying. Whatever it was.

And then the light dawned, when he was almost there, and he smacked his head. Idiot. It was nothing to do with him, or them. Not that there was a 'them' any more. It was about the books. She wanted to talk to him about the books, because she wanted to sell them.

Oh, well, he was there now.

He rang the bell and stepped back, and he saw a movement in the sitting room window. Millie, watching out for passers-by from the back of the sofa, her whole body wiggling in greeting just as she always did when she saw him.

She vanished, and he guessed Laura must be coming to the door. He braced himself, sucking in a long, slow breath and letting it out again. In again, nice and slow—hold—and out.

He saw a movement behind the glass, and the door swung slowly inwards.

'Tom.'

She looked—odd. Calm, composed, but odd, and his heart started to beat harder against his ribs.

'You left a message, saying you wanted to speak to me.'

She opened the door wider and stepped back, and he went in to a rapturous greeting from Millie, all wiggles and smiles as if nothing untoward was going on.

'Can I get you a drink?'

'No, I'm fine. What did you want? Is it about the books?'

She shook her head, and his mind went into overdrive.

'Tom, I can't do this standing in the hall. Come on in.'

She closed the front door, led him through to the kitchen and opened the fridge, getting out a bottle of chilled water and pouring herself a glass. 'Sure you don't want one?'

'Yes, I'm sure, I just had a coffee.' Come on, Laura, get to the point!

She put the water back into the fridge, closed the door and turned, propping herself against the worktop, arms wrapped around herself. He watched her chest rise slowly then fall as she took a calming breath, then she looked up and met his eyes.

'I'm pregnant.'

He felt the breath sucked out of his body, and pain swamped him.

No! Not that! Anything but that...

'No—no, Laura, you can't be. We...'

'I am. I have no idea how, but I am.' She picked up a white plastic wand off the windowsill and handed it to him, and he took it with nerveless fingers and stared at it, the word swimming in front of his eyes.

And there it was. The very last, very worst thing that should have happened. He could feel panic rising in his chest, the fear for his child overwhelming him.

'You can't. You can't be having a baby. We can't do this. This can't be happening.'

She folded her arms defensively across her chest and lifted her chin a fraction.

'I'm not asking anything of you, Tom. I don't need anything from you, you know I have more than enough money from my grandfather. I'm telling you because you have a right to know you're going to be a father. Whether or not you exercise that right is up to you, but I very much hope you will. I never had a father, and I would have loved one. I don't want my child to be denied that right—'

'You *can't* have it.'

Her chin firmed. 'Why not? Why can't I have it, Tom? It's my child, and not only *can* I have it, I *will* have it. This is happening.'

'No. Please, Laura, no. You don't understand.'

'Then tell me why. Make me understand, Tom, because frankly I don't.'

'Because I'm going *blind*, for the hundredth time, and it's hereditary!'

'I know that! And trust me, I didn't ask for this either, but we've made a baby, like it or not, and that's all there is to it.'

'No, it's not! I can't—I just—please, don't condemn it to this.'

'For that reason alone? Or because you don't want a child?'

'Of course I want a child!' he cried, his voice raw with anguish as he turned to face her, ravaged with grief. 'I'd love nothing more than to have this child, but I can't, Laura. We can't. I'm going to go blind, I won't be able to work, to drive, to look after it, to keep it safe, to do any of the things a father should be able to do. And worse than that, far, far worse than that is knowing that my child or my child's child would be sitting on a time bomb, waiting for the day when it can't see in the dark, when the light starts to close in, when it has no peripheral vision left, and then the rest breaks up until there's nothing, Laura. Nothing. Just darkness. Total, black, unrelieved darkness...'

His voice cracked, and she walked quietly over to him and put her hands on his face, but he couldn't meet her eyes. Not now...

'Look at me, Tom.'

He forced his eyes open and met her calm, level gaze.

'We can do this. Together—'

'No. No, we can't. I can't. Please, Laura, listen to me.'

'I am. I have. We've had this conversation, and I know how you feel. I feel the same, but we need to be rational. Your RP looks as if it's X-linked, which means your child won't go blind. If it's a boy, he won't even have the gene because he won't have your X chromosome, and if it's a girl, she will have it but she'll be a carrier. OK, she may have some symptoms, like your mother and grandmother, but by the time she's growing up there may well be a cure.'

'You don't know that. There may never be a cure.'

'No, but nor do you know there won't be. And as for you not being able to be a proper father, it could be years before your sight deteriorates to any significant extent, and even when it does, you can still be you. You can be a husband, a father, a doctor—you can be all of these things, and you can carry on doing them even when—if—you lose your sight. And your child will love you, Tom.'

Pain lanced through him, and he choked down a sob.

'Laura, you don't understand! If it's a girl, she could still have vision issues, and even if she didn't, it's just kicking the can down the road. You don't know there'll ever be a cure, and if she has a son he'll have this hanging over him like me. You can't wish that on them—or on any child.'

'Well, of course I don't wish it on anyone, who on earth would, but are you telling me that you shouldn't be here now? That you should have died before you were born because your life has been so worthless? What about all the people you've saved? Rob Wilding, for instance? That young man could be dead now if it hadn't been for you and the team you were leading, but instead he's going to be fine, and that's down to you. He owes you his life, and if your mother had done what you're suggesting I should do, he could be dead now and so could all the countless other people you've helped save over the past seven years. Ask your mother if she thinks that giving you life was the wrong thing to do. See what she says, because I'm sure she wouldn't agree.'

He looked away. 'Someone else would have saved them.'

'Tom! Stop it! You've made a huge difference to a lot of people in your life, and our child deserves the right to have the chance to do that, too, to grow up, to make a contribution to society, to be a part of the world. Not to allow that to happen on the strength of something that might or might not happen to them isn't fair, Tom, and I can't do it. I won't do it. I'm having this child, with you or without you, because I love it, and I love you, and I want to be with you and share this all with you, and there is no possible valid reason why that shouldn't happen.'

He shook his head, his eyes raw with grief. 'You still don't understand. I can't pass this on, Laura. I just can't. I couldn't live with myself.'

'You may not have done, but even if you

have, it really, really isn't the end of the world.' She took hold of his hands, pressed a kiss to them, held them against her heart and he could feel it beating.

'You're just scared, Tom,' she said gently, 'and it's OK to be scared, but you don't need to be. We can do this. Come on, sit down and let's have a drink. I'll make you a cup of tea and we can talk it over calmly.'

He shook his head and walked away, going into the sitting room with Millie at his heels. How could they do it? Together or otherwise, they couldn't change the course of destiny, and she was right, he *was* scared. And he'd never been this scared of anything in his life before.

He dropped onto the sofa, and Millie hopped up beside him and lay across his lap, her head against his chest, staring up into his eyes. He stroked her automatically, and she turned her head and licked his hand. To reassure him?

'Oh, Millie. Are you really clever enough to keep someone safe? How do you do that?'

Her tail waved, and he smiled in spite of himself.

* * *

'Here, your tea. Don't let her jog your arm.'

She set it down beside him, curled up at the other end of the sofa and watched him thoughtfully.

He was stroking Millie, and just that simple action seemed to be calming him.

'How did she do it?' he asked, his voice a little gruff.

'Guide him? Years of training,' she said quietly. 'They're bred for their calm reliability, their intelligence, their gentleness and trustworthiness. That's important because they also have to be big, so they can do the things they have to do, like block your path.'

'Block it?'

'Yes. If you're going to walk into danger, they're trained to cross in front of you and stop, so you can't go any further. She did it with me on the day of our interview.'

'With you?' He looked confused. 'How? Why?'

She smiled a little sadly. 'Because I was miles away, walking along without paying attention, and a car was reversing out of a drive. She blocked me, and probably saved me from

'Ok, hang on a minute. Supposing you re-member you want something from here. Grumps used to shop here. Just say, "Millie, paper shop,"' Laura said, so he did, and Mil-lie turned towards the paper shop and stopped at the door.

He laughed. 'She's amazing.'

'She is amazing. She's also a lovely, lovely friend. Grumps said it was almost worth los-ing his sight just to have her, because she was such good company.' She smiled up at him, her eyes gentle, loving. 'Shall we go home now?' she asked, and he felt something start to bloom in his chest. Something bright and beautiful that felt remarkably like hope.

He smiled back. 'Yes. Yes, let's do that. Mil-lie, go home,' he said, and—only for a few seconds—he closed his eyes and let her lead him. And he got feedback through the han-dle, the sway of her back as she walked, the slightest change of pace, the detour around an obstacle. He opened his eyes and found they were almost at the door, and as soon as they were in he took the harness off and gave her a massive cuddle.

'You are such a clever girl,' he said proudly,

and she rolled on her back and beamed up at him, tail swooshing. 'Hussy,' he murmured, and Laura laughed.

'Come on. It's time for her lunchtime biscuit. When did you last eat? Did you have breakfast?'

He shrugged. 'I don't remember.'

'Right. Let's have some lunch, and we can talk some more.'

'I'd rather go to bed. I just want to hold you. I've missed you so much, and I've been so...'

'Unhappy?' she finished for him, and he nodded.

'Yes. I knew I couldn't ever be with you, and the thought of that was killing me. And now...'

'You can be with me, Tom. Always. Come on. Let's settle Millie, then, and go to bed. I could really do with a cuddle, too.'

CHAPTER NINE

'I'VE MISSED YOU so much this week,' he said, cradling her against his body and letting her warmth thaw the cold, dark place inside him.

'I've missed you, too. I've been so worried about you, you've been so odd.'

'I felt odd. Dislocated and lost. And now this—what a seesaw. I can't believe you're pregnant. How long have you known?'

'Since this morning. Well, that's when I did the test, but I've had my suspicions for a few days.'

He frowned. 'And you didn't tell me? Why? How could you keep that a secret from me?'

'That coming from you?' She smiled sadly at him and touched his face with a gentle hand. 'Because I knew just how you'd react.'

'And I did. I'm sorry. I might have known you'd knock down any barriers I tried to put up between us. I always knew you'd put me first and yourself last, because that's what you always do.'

'You make it sound like a failing,' she murmured, and he laughed softly and kissed her.

'No, it's not a failing, but I wasn't going to let you do that, so I couldn't be with you no matter how much I wanted to be. I was desperate to be here, but that was just selfish and self-indulgent.'

'It's not self-indulgent,' she said, cradling his face in her hand. 'We can do this, you know. It will be OK.'

'Will it?' He let his hand slide down and come to rest in the bowl of her pelvis, still flat of course so early on. 'I wonder what it is. I hope it's a boy, so I don't have to live with a guilty conscience for the rest of my life.'

'You don't. You've got nothing to feel guilty about, Tom. Whatever happens, we'll have a child who's loved.'

'How soon can they tell the sex? Is it about sixteen weeks?'

'Something like that. I think you can sometimes tell at fourteen weeks, but does it make any difference, Tom? I mean, if we found out at a scan that the baby would have Down's, or a congenital heart condition, or missing limbs or spina bifida—what would you want to do?'

It stopped his thoughts in their tracks. He'd been obsessed by the eye condition, but she was right, there were worse things, things that would make far more difference to their child's health and well-being, but they'd still want to have that child, still love it every bit as much, still fight for it with every last ounce of strength they could muster.

He smiled sadly. 'You know the answer to that. I don't want you not to have this baby, Laura, of course I don't. I was just gutted for it, I wasn't expecting it, and I panicked. It was a knee-jerk reaction. But you're right, it won't be affected in the same way as me, and yes, there might be a cure by the time it's relevant. But I'd still rather it was a boy so I don't have to feel guilty.'

'You're such a softy,' she said with a smile, and she leant over and kissed him. 'Make love to me, Tom. I've missed you.'

'I've missed you, too. Come here.'

* * *

They talked for hours, lying there in each other's arms, until hunger finally drove them out of bed and into the kitchen.

She made a stack of sandwiches and they ate them on the sofa with Millie between them eyeing them longingly, and then they took her for a run on the cliff then back to his house to collect overnight things because there was no way they were going to be apart if she had anything to do with it.

He'd been alone enough dealing with this, and like it or not, she was going to be there for him from now on, come hell or high water.

Assuming he wanted that, but he still hadn't said he loved her. Maybe she was making assumptions?

She sat cross-legged in the middle of the bed and watched him as he pulled out some clothes and put them in a bag. Not many, just enough for tomorrow. What about the next day, and the next? What about the future? Did they even have one?

'What are we going to do about this, Tom?' she asked quietly, suddenly realising that she had no idea where they were heading.

He stopped what he was doing and looked at her, puzzled.

'About what?'

'Us. You and me. Are you going to carry on living here and spending the odd night with me, or are we going to live together, or what?'

He sat down on the side of the bed next to her and took her hand in his. 'I don't know,' he said, his voice gruff. He looked down at their hands, his face guarded. 'At one point you used the word "husband". Did you mean that, or was it just...?'

'No. No, I meant it. If it's what you want.'

He searched her eyes. 'Are you asking me to marry you? Because I don't want you doing that just because of the baby.'

'I'm not.'

His mouth tipped into a wry, uncertain smile. 'Not asking me to marry you, or not doing it because of the baby?'

She laughed a little tearfully. 'Not doing it because of the baby, you idiot. Or because you might go blind, but because I love you. I've told you that so many times now, but I still don't know how you feel, and I don't what you want from me, what you want from us. I need to know.'

His smile said it all. 'Of course I love you, Laura. You must know that.'

'I don't. You've never told me.'

'Well, I should have done. I probably should have done it years ago. I've loved you since the day I met you, but you didn't want to know. I even had the crazy idea that if I put myself about a bit you'd get jealous, but it just drove you further away. I can't tell you how sorry I am about that, about the wasted years we could have been together, the time we could have spent getting to know each other properly.'

'We probably weren't ready then. And you were right, all the moving around you do as a junior doctor is very disruptive. It might have ruined it, been too much of a strain on our relationship.'

'And now?'

She smiled and cradled his jaw in her hand, loving the feel of stubble against her palm, the raw masculinity so in contrast to his gentleness. Or maybe not. They weren't either/or things.

'I think we're ready now,' she said. 'So—

will you? Will you marry me? For better, for worse, for richer, for poorer... We'll ignore the next bit.'

His smile warmed his eyes, setting off the little creases and softening his features. He turned his face into her hand and kissed it, then looked back at her.

'Yes, Laura. I will marry you, willingly. As soon as you like. Because I love you more than I have words for. I can't— I'm not—'

She laid a finger over his lips and cut him off. 'Shh. You don't need to find flowery words, Tom. Just a simple "I love you" is all I need to hear. All I'll ever need to hear.'

'Good, because I can probably manage that,' he said with a rueful smile, and he leant over her and kissed her. 'I love you.'

'Love you, too. You'd better pack a bit more stuff.'

They walked into the ED together the following day, his arm round her shoulders, and she felt eyes swivel towards them. Lots of eyes.

'Well, you two look a bit happier,' James said drily, and she could feel Tom's chuckle.

'Yeah. Sorry about that. Actually, we have some good news. We're getting married.'

There was a flurry of good wishes, and Livvy flung her arms around Laura and kissed her.

'I'm so happy for you,' she said, and Laura found herself laughing and crying and feeling a little foolish.

'Sorry, this isn't very professional,' she said, swiping tears, but James was grinning and all the patients in earshot were smiling, and it was lovely.

'So when's the big day?' Livvy asked when it had all died down a bit, and Laura shrugged.

'Not yet. Soon, but not yet. We haven't even had time to think about it, never mind plan it, but—it will be soon.'

'You are, aren't you?' Livvy whispered, and Laura gave up any hope of keeping it a secret and nodded.

'Yes. Yes, I am. Only just, and that isn't why we're getting married. We do love each other.'

'I would never have known,' Livvy said drily, and Laura chuckled.

'Am I that transparent?'

'Pretty much. So how's the queasy thing?'

'Ugh. We might not have the wedding for another couple of months, just so I can enjoy it. It's only going to be really small, but I'd love you to be there.'

Livvy hugged her again. 'That would be fabulous. Thank you. And if you want any help planning it...'

'I'll ask,' she said with a smile. 'Now I'd better go and talk to James.'

'Yes, because of X-rays and stuff in Resus. I have to go out every time, and sometimes that's quite difficult. I think I might end up in Minors permanently soon, or just in cubicles. Something less challenging.' And then her face fell. 'Oh, no, you won't be taking my job! James'll be gutted.'

She smiled. 'No, he won't. He's an old romantic. And anyway, you might change your mind and decide motherhood's not all it's cracked up to be,' she said with a laugh, but Livvy shook her head.

'No. I want to be at home for Amber and Charlie anyway. I love spending time with them. But maybe he'll be able to hold the job open for you to come back when you're ready. You never know, you might change your mind and decide motherhood's not all it's cracked up to be,' Livvy quoted back at her, and then walked away with a cheeky grin.

She felt Tom's hand slide into hers and squeeze it. 'Come with me. I'm going to talk to James now. He's in his office.'

'OK.'

Telling James was easier than he'd expected, and his reaction was calm and reasoned.

'Are your eyes still OK to work at the moment?'

'Yes, absolutely—well, as long as the lights don't go out.'

'In which case I think we might all have a problem, so I'll have a word with Maintenance,' he said with a smile. 'Just—say if you need any help, or time off for appointments, anything like that. Or time off for the wedding, come to that. When is it?'

They looked at each other and shrugged.

'Soon,' Tom said firmly.

'Not too soon. I want to be able to enjoy it.' She looked her boss firmly in the eye and smiled. 'I might need a few concessions. I'm having a baby.'

James's smile widened, and he got up from behind his desk, came round and hugged her hard.

'That's such lovely news, Laura. I'm so pleased for you both.'

'Are you? I thought you had me lined up for Livvy's job?'

He chuckled and propped himself on the edge of the desk. 'Well, I did, and it'll still be there, of course. Technically she can hand in her notice any time up to two months before the end of her maternity leave, so if you wanted to apply at that point we'd be delighted to talk to you about it. And we could rig your shifts so they didn't overlap too badly. Or you could work part-time, or job-share with Livvy if she wanted to do that. You may not want to, of course. Connie didn't, and we don't need the money, so it suits us, but it doesn't suit everyone. Just keep in touch when the time comes. And for now, take all necessary precautions in Resus and around the department, and look after yourself.'

She nodded. 'Thank you.'

'Don't thank me, just invite me to the wedding.'

'Oh, don't worry, you're on the list. If it wasn't for you bending the rules after he'd missed the application deadline, it wouldn't be happening.'

'Are you saying this is my fault?' James said with a chuckle, and slapped Tom on the back. 'Go on, both of you, go and get on with some work before I change my mind and do something evil to the rota.'

Two hours later he was coming out of a cubicle when she spotted a young man in a wheelchair trundling towards her, being pushed by his parents. She didn't recognise him, but she recognised the injuries—the left leg propped up with an ex-fix scaffold on it, the right arm in a cast. At least this time he wasn't covered in blood, and she greeted them all with a smile.

'Rob. It's good to meet you at last. I'm Laura. Wow. You look so well! Hang on, let me get Tom.'

She popped her head into Resus. 'Have you got a minute?'

'Yeah, sure, I was just finishing up some notes. What's up?'

'Nothing. There's someone who wants to see you. Someone to justify your existence,' she added with a smile.

He frowned and followed her out, then laughed softly.

'Well, look at you. That's amazing. How are you, Rob?'

'I'm good,' he said. 'Bit sore still here and there, but I'm getting better. They're sending me home, but I just wanted to meet you and say thanks. They said you saved my life.'

'There were a lot of us involved, Rob. Not just us.'

'I know, but—they talked about it upstairs. How lucky I'd been. They said my hand was turned right over.'

Tom nodded. 'It was. How is it? Does it work? Can you feel it?'

'Yeah, it works. I can't feel the outside of my little finger a lot, and my grip's pretty rubbish, but I can nearly hold a pen now and I can use my phone.'

'Oh, well, that's all right then,' Tom said with a chuckle. 'Get your priorities right. How about your legs?'

He pulled a face. 'My right leg's OK, my left

leg—well, you can see that. I've got this gross thing on it for another three weeks at least, and then they might put a cast on it for a bit longer, but they think I should be able to start weight bearing again in a couple of months.'

'Yeah, it could take a while, but it's great you're making so much progress. Thank you for coming to see us. It's really good to see you again. You take care—and no more biking!'

'No way,' he said, pulling a face. 'Never again. I've learned that lesson properly. Thanks. Really, thanks.'

He was welling up a bit, so they gave him some space and talked to his parents for a moment, then waved him off.

'That was nice of them.'

Tom raised an eyebrow. 'He still looks pretty broken. I reckon he'll have trouble with that left leg off and on for a long while, if not for life.'

'But he has it, and he has his right hand, and he's still breathing and talking and thinking clearly. I would say that's a win.'

'Absolutely.' He hugged her, then let her go. 'I need to get back into Resus. Are you OK?'

She smiled. 'I'm fine. Livvy's got the bit between her teeth. We're talking weddings.'

He rolled his eyes, said, 'Enjoy!' and went back into Resus.

They got married two months later, in early July, and it was a glorious day, warm and sunny but not too hot, with a light breeze to cool them and the scent of roses in the air.

The wedding was held in the grounds of the hotel where Tom had stayed on the night of the interview. It seemed an appropriate choice, and it also came recommended by Livvy as she and Matt had got married there two years ago.

It was a simple ceremony, held under the shelter of a delicately pretty white wrought-iron gazebo, and their few, carefully chosen guests were seated on chairs on the lawn in front of them.

His parents Katherine and Mike were there, of course, still coming to terms with his diagnosis but thrilled about the wedding and the baby, and Livvy and Matt, James and Connie, and Ryan and Beth, who was holding their little son Raoul, and after the ceremony they had a champagne afternoon tea, with alcohol-free sparkling wine for Laura and Livvy, and it was perfect.

They'd decided not to have any speeches, but then Tom suddenly got to his feet and tapped his wine glass with a spoon.

'You thought you'd got away with that, didn't you?' he said, and they all laughed. 'I just couldn't let today go by without a few thank-yous. First and foremost, to my parents, who've put up with a lot from me for very many years now, and are probably more than happy to pass the baton to Laura. I wouldn't be here without you and your unfailing support, so thank you both, from the bottom of my heart.'

Katherine was welling up, and Mike coughed and nodded and handed her a tissue, and Tom went on.

'So—James. This is actually your fault. If you hadn't interviewed me for the job, I wouldn't have seen Laura again, and if you hadn't kept her on as a locum as long as you have, we wouldn't have worked together, which gave us a chance to build bridges and recon-nect with each other. So thank you, for inad-vertently throwing us together. We owe you.'

He looked down at Laura, and her heart turned over.

'And then there's Laura, the only woman I've ever really loved. Laura, who turned me down so many times while we were at uni, who so nearly changed her mind but then didn't, who really didn't want me here at first. I stole her job, then I stole her heart—although apparently I'd already done that and she'd failed to tell me.'

That caused a chuckle, as it was meant to, and then he got serious.

'It's only fair, she stole mine years ago, and now I can't get rid of her, even though I tried, because she's got guts, this wife of mine. I don't know how many of you know this, but at some point in the future, I'm going to start to lose my sight. Any woman in her right mind would run a mile from that, but not my Laura, oh, no. She stayed, she became my rock. She taught me not to be afraid, and in her own inimitable way she told me, and I quote, "Looking on the bright side, at least you won't be able to see my wrinkles."'

He waited for the ripple of laughter to die down, and then went on with a smile, 'With a love like that to see me through, I know we'll make it, and no matter how old we grow together, whatever that brings, I'll always have the memory of how beautiful she looks today. Thank you, my love, with all my heart, for everything.'

His voice cracked a little, and he reached out a hand and drew her up into his arms and kissed her, and she rested her head on his shoulder and blinked away the tears.

'I love you,' she murmured. 'It's going to be wonderful bringing up our family and growing old with you by my side, whatever it throws at us. You're the best thing that's ever happened to me, and our baby's going to be the luckiest child in the world.'

She went up on tiptoe and kissed him, and then laughed as the others clustered round them and they were showered with rose petals.

She picked a rose petal off his eyelashes and met his eyes. 'Time to go home to Millie?'

He smiled. 'I think so.'

They walked home—to her home, because they'd decided to keep it for themselves and let his cottage once it was done up—and Katherine and Mike walked back with them and then parted company at the gate. They were staying in his cottage, and he said he'd call them in the morning and maybe they could have breakfast together, and then he paused at her front door after they'd waved them off, unlocked the door and scooped Laura up in his arms.

'Are you carrying me over the threshold?' she said with a little giggle, and he grinned.

'Absolutely. Got to do these things properly.'

'Like your speech?' she said as he put her down and gave Millie a cuddle.

He looked up and smiled. 'I had to say something. I meant every word, by the way.'

'What, even the suggestion that I'm not in my right mind?'

He laughed and pulled her into his arms, and she rested her head on his chest with a quiet sigh. 'We'll be all right,' he said softly. 'You, me, the baby.'

'Don't forget Millie.'

He looked down at the dog, sitting at their feet and wagging her tail hopefully, and he smiled.

'As if I could ever forget Millie...'

* * * * *

LET'S TALK

Romance

For exclusive extracts, competitions
and special offers, find us online:

- **f** facebook.com/millsandboon
- ⓘ @millsandboonuk
- 🐦 @millsandboon

Or get in touch on 0844 844 1351*

For all the latest titles coming soon,
visit millsandboon.co.uk/nextmonth

Want even more
ROMANCE?

Join our bookclub today!

'Mills & Boon books, the perfect way to escape for an hour or so.'

Miss W. Dyer

'Excellent service, promptly delivered and very good subscription choices.'

Miss A. Pearson

'You get fantastic special offers and the chance to get books before they hit the shops'

Mrs V. Hall

Visit millsandbook.co.uk/Bookclub and save on brand new books.

MILLS & BOON